REFUGIO'S GOLD

By Major Mitchell
&
Jerry Mitchell

Shalako Press
P.O. Box 371
Oakdale, CA 95361

ISBN: 978-0-9908878-8-1

For information contact: Shalako Press
P.O. Box 371, Oakdale, CA 95361-0371
http://www.shalakopress.com

Cover design: Karen Borrelli
Editor: Judith Mitchell
Cover photograph of Amy Ruiz taken by Wiley Joiner

Acknowledgments

Like all books, this book is a combined effort of many people.

We would like to thank Judy Mitchell for her many edits that turn our scribbles into something readable.

We would also like to thank Steve Haak and Gary Crawford for their reviews and for catching additional errors.

A big thanks to historian Wiley Joiner for the loan of the antique shotgun seen on the front cover. Wiley also took multiple photographs for Karen to use on the cover.

A huge thank you to Amy Ruiz, who agreed to dress in period costume and allow herself to be photographed for the cover. She is living proof that nice girls also like guns.

As always, we stop to thank Karen Borrelli for creating an attractive cover.

Most of all, hugs and kisses to our wives, Judy and Juana, who not only allow, but support our writing habits. We love you, ladies.

Dedication

This book is lovingly dedicated to Judy and Juana, who allow us to keep the traditions of the old west alive.

Refugio's Gold

Clay woke before sunrise and eased himself toward the edge of the bed, careful not to disturb Teresa lying beside him. He pulled on his boots as she moaned softly and squirmed deeper under the blanket. Antonio, Teresa's big yellow dog, yawned and stretched himself as Clay grabbed his hat from the bedpost. Patting Antonio on the head, he opened the door and slipped into the early morning air.

A tinge of dust hung in the cool morning breeze, left over from the strong wind which had swept through Carrizo Springs the night before. He kicked at the sand piled against the outhouse door before pulling it open. Antonio had his leg hiked against one of the fence posts when he appeared seconds later, and Teresa's rooster emerged from the henhouse to flap his wings and crow. It was going to be another hot day with no sign of rain. They were well into the third year of drought, and if it didn't rain soon, Clay was certain the entire state of Texas was going to turn to dust and blow into Mexico.

He drew a bucket of water from the well, taking note that he had to let out several inches more rope than he had several days ago. He built a fire and filled the coffee pot before scrubbing his face and hands in a wash basin. He dumped water into a clay bowl for Antonio and tossed the dog a few stale tortillas left from last night's supper. Clay filled his favorite mug, then slipped quietly back inside and sat in the chair, staring at the woman in his bed. One long, shapely limb had slipped from the blanket and her dark brown hair filled the pillow. He still didn't know how he'd been lucky enough to marry her. She was only half his age and far too pretty for the likes of him. But after her repeated professions of love, Clay quit fighting and took her to the priest. They were married inside the small church next to the cemetery.

He had been married to June for nearly twenty years, and had always wondered how a God-fearing Methodist woman could put up with him that long. Her death was a crushing blow, and he had sworn that he'd never find another woman. They had never had children, which was a huge burden in itself, but he was a lawman, and had shot a number of men and hung several others. While she never mentioned it, he knew it bothered her, especially when he came home drunk after having killed a man.

He guessed he'd never have to worry about Teresa when it came to things like that. He'd seen her strap the matching pearl-handled .38s against her slender hips on more than one occasion, and knew how quickly she could draw and fire either weapon. While he'd only seen June take a nip of brandy on a cold winter day, Teresa could down a glass of tequila and pour another without blinking an eye. Making love to June was tender and sweet, sort of like being married to an honest-to-God angel. The first night with Teresa, however, was wild and playful. They were different in most every way he could think of. The only conclusion he could land on, while watching her sleep, was that he loved each woman equally.

She stretched her lean body with a soft moan and smiled at him.

"*Por que, mi marido.* Are you sorry you married me?"

"Are you kidding?" Clay sat on the edge of the bed and handed her the mug of coffee. "I was just thinking how lucky I was."

"Mmm," she took a sip and grinned, "I'm the lucky one. I used to bring Refugio his coffee in bed. Now, I'm the one with a husband who brings me coffee." She kissed him before taking another sip.

"That's 'cause he never knew how special you are."

"No, you are the special one." She pulled his head down for another kiss.

"It's gonna be hotter than Hades out there today. If we're going to get your gold, we'd best be heading out."

"*Si.*" She handed him the mug before tossing the blanket aside. He cursed himself as she slipped her nightgown over her nude body and headed toward the door.

The damned gold could've waited another day, you numbskull. Feeling Teresa's body against his suddenly seemed more important than a chest full of gold.

Chapter 2

Sixteen-year-old Roberta Sawyer finished tossing table scraps to the hogs and used her apron to wipe the sweat from her forehead. It wasn't quite noon and the sun had already begun baking the Texas prairie. The few blades of grass left were brown and brittle, not fit to feed their horses or mules. Her mother had been badgering her father to pack up and move back to Tennessee while the animals were strong enough to pull a wagon, but papa kept arguing that the drought couldn't last forever. "The rain is sure to come any day now," he insisted. Roberta studied the steel-blue sky without seeing a single cloud anywhere. *Ain't likely to rain for a month of Sundays, Daddy. From the look of things, we'll dry up and blow away before that happens.* Theodore Rolling had asked for her hand in marriage, and had been talking about an October wedding, after the weather turned cool. His father owned the general store in Carrizo Springs, and she'd been trying to persuade him to have a summer wedding so she could get off this God-forsaken farm and move to town.

She was about to enter the house when she saw the riders. There were close to twenty, all bunched up and walking their horses toward their farm.

"Riders coming, Pa. A whole passel of 'em," she yelled. Her father used his hand to shade his eyes for a few seconds.

"Get your ma and get inside. Now!"

Roberta darted toward the back of the house where her mother was doing laundry. "Riders coming, Ma. Pa says for us to get inside, now!"

The riders were almost to the corral when they reached the front door, where her father was shoving shells into his Henry rifle.

"What is it, George?" her mother said.

"Might be wrong, but I'm guessing it's the bunch that's been raiding ranches.

"Lord have mercy," her mother said as she grabbed the .36 caliber pistol hanging by the door. Roberta began shoving shells into the double-barreled shotgun as her father stepped out onto the porch.

"What are you fellers looking for? This is private property." He raised the rifle to his shoulder, but the first shot hit him in the chest, knocking him against the side of the house. The Henry rattled harmlessly across the porch as he fell. Her mother screamed and bolted through the door. Three more shots caused her to fall next to her husband.

Roberta shook uncontrollably as tears blinded her eyes. She cocked both hammers on the twelve-gauge and braced herself against the back wall of the living room. The first man through the door was propelled backward to the porch as she pulled the first trigger. The second met a similar fate when she pulled the other trigger. The next three jerked the gun away as she tried desperately to reload. They hit her repeatedly in the face, then ripped her clothes from her body. She was pinned nude to the floor and held by four laughing, leering men while a fifth lowered his pants and climbed on top of her.

"Oh God, no! Please no!" she begged, but her words only made them laugh harder. They took turns abusing her as the men outside shot the hogs and tied their carcasses on the horses and mules. Roberta was finally dragged naked through the door where she saw the bodies of her parents without their scalps. Someone was setting fire to the barn as she was forced onto the back of one of the horses. One of the men grabbed the reins and pulled her horse forward into line with the rest. She glanced once toward the burning barn, then back toward the dirty man in front of her. The world began to fade, and Roberta rode without seeing or feeling.

Chapter 3

"Miguel has mules at the stables in Carrizo Springs," Teresa said with a scowl as she urged Diablo next to Loco. "Why are we going out of the way to buy mules from Sawyer when we could already have them?"

"Because, wife of mine," Clay grinned at her slant-wise, "what Miguel has are scrawny little burros, not honest-to-god Tennessee plow mules. What Sawyer has are almost as big as these horses we're riding, and they'll carry a full load all day long without tiring."

"Burros are humble, sacred animals," Teresa said with pouty lips. "They are what our Lord Jesus rode."

"Yeah, they are fine critters in their own right, but maybe the Lord don't mind us using something different, especially since we're going after the gold Refugio stole from the Mexican government. We ain't exactly figuring on giving it back, are we?"

"No, at least I'm not. What is it?" she said as Clay brought Loco to a halt and grabbed her arm.

"I don't know, but I don't like the looks of this." He pointed toward the smoke ascending upward and the buzzards circling in the sky. She quickly checked the loads in the twin .38s as Clay drew his Winchester from the scabbard. They walked their horses over the rise and stopped to stare at the empty corral and charred remains of the barn that belonged to George Sawyer.

"*Santa María, madre de Dios,*" Teresa said, crossing her breast.

"You can say that again. Let's go have a closer look-see, but put that pistol away and pull yer rifle. If they're still around, it ain't likely they'll let us close enough to use a handgun." Clay urged Loco forward at a walk. Teresa pulled the Winchester and followed, keeping just behind her husband and to the right. It wasn't until they saw the bodies of George and Martha that she burst into tears.

"Best keep your wits about you, 'till we make sure they've gone," Clay said, dismounting.

He ducked inside the house and returned seconds later shaking his head.

"Ain't no one inside."

Teresa looked up from where she was kneeling beside Martha's body and wiped her eyes with the back of her gloved hand. "Where's the *niña*? They have a daughter, no?"

"She ain't in the house. I'll take a look-see, but I don't figure on finding her."

"*Por qué?*"

"Bastards more'n likely took her. Best find something to cover them up before the buzzards get 'em," he added as Teresa cursed loudly in Spanish.

He returned minutes later after scouting about the house and stables. Teresa had both bodies covered with blankets from their bedrolls.

"They left nothing inside to cover them," she said without his asking.

"I know. They're like a bunch of locusts, except a locust will leave the barn standing." He wiped the sweat from his brow and adjusted his hat. "Come on, we'd best take them inside so the buzzards and coyotes won't have a feast while we fetch Ray. I reckon he'll want to know about this."

"Shouldn't one of us stay with them," Teresa said in a strained voice as they carried George Sawyer's body inside.

"Uh-uh." Clay shook his head as he headed toward the door. "I ain't leaving you here alone while them renegades are running around, and I'm certainly not sending you to Carrizo Springs by your lonesome either, so get that notion out of you head right now."

"*Sí*, but I'm a big girl. I can take care of myself."

"That ain't the issue." He took her face between his palms. "I know you can take care of yourself. I just want you around to take care of me. Understand?"

"*Sí*, if you put it that way, I'll go with you," she said with a shrug as she grabbed Martha Sawyer's legs. "We'll go to town together. I thought you were a big boy."

"I am. I'm just a lot better with you by my side." Clay backed through the door and placed Martha beside her husband.

Chapter 4

Sheriff Ray King looked up from the newspaper he was reading as Clay held the door open for Teresa. "Howdy, Clay. I thought you two were leaving town for a couple of weeks."

"We were. That is, until we found George and Martha Sawyer all cut to pieces, their barn burnt and the livestock missing."

"What?" Ray let the newspaper slip through his fingers to the floor as he stood. "When was this? What about Roberta?"

"We found them just a little before noon. Got here as soon as we could, and Roberta's missing. I figure they carried her off like a pack of coyotes. They scalped them, Ray."

"You keep saying *they*. Who you figuring done it?"

"Your guess is as good as mine. Me and Teresa think it might've been Comancheros, or some other renegades making it look like their handiwork. I figure they hadn't been gone too long when we arrived. The barn was still smoking."

"We need to find the *niña*," Teresa snapped.

"Yes, ma'am, I figure on doing just that, as soon as I get a posse together." Ray grabbed his gun belt from a peg near the door and paused with a crooked grin. "By the way, I've got a friend of yours locked in a cell. He claims you can vouch for him." He finished buckling the gun belt and opened the door separating the office from the cells. Clay stared as a young vaquero sat upright on one of the cots.

"That's Julio Garcia," Clay said with a nod. "Yeah, I know him. What have you got him locked up for?"

"A fellow named Luke Warren swore out a complaint against him. He said Julio threatened him with a gun. Reckon I'm supposed to arrest you and Teresa also, according to him, but I figured on asking a few questions before trying something like that. Any truth to what the man says?"

"I don't know what he said, but I doubt there's a lot of truth in whatever it was. First of all, Julio don't make threats. If he pulled an iron on that fat sonofabitch, he'd be pushing up daisies instead of trying to stir up trouble. I'm surprised he let you arrest him."

"I was too. He just handed me his gun and said I should talk to you. I figured there was more to it than what Luke was saying. Why don't you give me your side of the story?" Julio gave Clay a silent nod as the sheriff turned away.

"It was back when we was looking for Ruth Bishop, Lester's granddaughter. Teresa was healing after getting shot in the shoulder, and the heat was getting to her. We stopped at his sorry excuse of a bar, just wanting to get out of the sun and get a drink of water. Then he starts calling Teresa names and says we ain't welcome. I'm the one who pulled the gun, and I was fixin' to make a pig trough outta his skull when Teresa stopped me. Then we moseyed down the road and stopped at Guillermo's cantina. We were eating dinner when that fat bastard shows up with three men claiming to be lawmen, wanting to arrest us. That's when everyone in the place got involved, and Julio didn't pull no gun. He didn't need to. Teresa saved Luke Warren's bacon that time too."

"I will not do it again," Teresa said with a shake of her head.

"Well, I reckon it can wait until we bury George and Martha, and find their daughter." Ray grabbed his hat and adjusted it by giving the brim a tug.

"You might think about turning Julio loose, and giving him his hardware," Clay said. "We're going to need fellers who can shoot."

Ray stared at him for a second before grabbing the keys from the drawer. "Not a bad idea."

~   ~   ~

It took Ray about an hour to gather a posse of eight, counting himself, Clay, Teresa and Julio. Theodore Rolling had insisted on coming, but Clay figured the young man wasn't going to be much help, and would need someone to look out after him when the shooting started. They escorted a buckboard with three heavily armed men to the Sawyer ranch, where they loaded the bodies into the wagon.

"Okay," Ray said as the buckboard rattled its way toward town, "everyone get some rest for the next couple of hours. We'll be leaving at sunset and traveling by night. The way I figure is, they'll make camp somewhere, and if we move fast, we'll gain some ground on 'em. Make sure your horse is watered and rested also."

Clay spread a blanket on the porch for Teresa and lay beside her, but sleep failed to come. He kept seeing George and Martha's bodies. He had Loco and Diablo saddled by the time Ray gave the call to make ready.

~   ~   ~

Julio Garcia took the lead, following their tracks by lantern. The posse moved quietly, walking their horses at a fast pace. They had only covered five miles, by Clay's calculation, when they smelled wood smoke and roasting meat. Julio motioned them to stop, then dismounted and crept forward to peer through a clump of greasewoods at the top of a small rise. The vaquero pointed toward Ray and Clay, and motioned them forward.

"Having themselves a damned party," Ray whispered as he peeked through the greasewood. The men below were roasting one of Sawyer's hogs while they drank and took liberties with the young girl in the center of the clearing.

"Why not? It usually takes folks a few days, maybe even weeks to discover what they've done. By that time, they're long gone. It just so happened that Teresa and me came along. How do you want to play this?"

"Well, you, Teresa and Julio are probably the best at this game. I'd like you to mosey around and close the back door. I don't want any of the sons of bitches getting away, if we can help it."

"Give us fifteen minutes before you open the ball." Clay grabbed Ray's arm as he turned away. "Don't let Ted see what they're doing to Roberta. We've got enough on our plate as it is."

Ray nodded, and Clay motioned Julio toward the left as he and Teresa scampered hunched-over toward the right. They had almost reached position when a man's screams, followed by gunshots, pierced their ears. Clay turned to see Theodore Rolling running toward the bandits, yelling and shooting a pistol.

Chapter 5

"Dammit!" Clay yelled. "Stick here and shoot anyone who tries to escape."

Teresa ran twenty yards farther and took a position behind a boulder. She cringed as the gang sent a volley of bullets that dropped Theodore in his tracks. She glanced to the right as Clay cursed loudly and fired his rifle, dropping one of the bandits. Teresa followed suit by firing several times, killing one horse and wounding one man, who grabbed his leg and sought cover behind the fallen animal. She worked her way closer as the thieves scrambled for their horses. The entire posse was now firing at will. She dropped to one knee and took careful aim. Her shot took out a man with long dark hair and a red bandana as he charged for an exit. A shot from the far side of the clearing took another from the saddle.

"Good shot, Julio," Teresa said, and fired again. The number of bandits was thinning rapidly. She pulled the trigger and the hammer fell on an empty chamber, so she tucked herself tightly behind another boulder to reload. Three gang members cut the rope picketing the mules and horses, and charged them toward her position, shooting and yelling. A shot from Clay's gun knocked one of the men from his horse, and a shot from the posse took the horse from under a second. Teresa dropped her rifle and pulled a pistol, firing as the third man went flying past. He dropped his gun and hunched over the horse, holding his left arm.

The battle was suddenly quiet, and Teresa rose cautiously, surveying the battlefield through a haze of gun smoke. Dead and dying bandits were lying everywhere, but Sawyer's mules and most of the horses were gone. She jerked around as Clay sprinted toward her.

"You okay? I saw that turkey trying to shoot you."

"*Sí,* and I shot him, but did not kill him." She shook her head and finished reloading the rifle.

"But you're okay? You're not hurt in any way?"

"*Sí,*" she giggled, "I am fine. I will show you later when we get somewhere private." She stood on her tiptoes to give him a peck on the lips.

"That might take time. Looks like we're going to have plenty of company tonight," Clay said as Ray King and several men approached.

"At least two made it out the backside before you got a chance to cover them," Ray said.

"Yeah, and Teresa wounded a third who made it out that way. What happened? I thought you were going to give me some time," Clay growled.

"Ted went crazy when he saw what they were doing to Roberta. I told Jess to keep an eye on him, but Ted whacked him with his gun and went charging their camp."

Clay glanced toward Jess Walker, where the middle-aged man was sitting on a rock, holding a bloody handkerchief to his head.

"Is he going to be okay?"

"Yeah, but he might need a couple of stitches when we get back to town."

"I'll take a look at it," Teresa said, squatting in front of the man and gently removing the handkerchief.

"Didn't do Ted much good," Ray said, squatting beside her. "He's deader'n last year's daisies."

"That will not make his mother and father happy," Teresa said as she washed the wound with water from a canteen. "I will say prayers for them and their son."

"I'll make sure to tell them," Ray said. "But I did hear him say once that he loved Roberta more'n anything, and wished he could be by her side forever."

"From the looks of Roberta, he might be getting his wish." Clay's voice trailed off as Julio knelt beside Roberta and gently wrapped her in a saddle blanket, then picked her up and carried her to a comfortable clearing near the top of the hill. "Kind of makes you wonder, don't it?"

"What does?" Ray said.

"Him." He motioned toward Julio. "He'd just as soon shoot your eye out as to look at most people. Now, he's acting like a nurse. Wonder what made him like that?"

"Don't know, and I don't plan on asking. I'm just glad we had his gun on this deal." Ray turned to yell at the posse.

"Best make camp back over the other side of the hill, unless y'all want to sleep with a bunch of dead highbinders."

"What do you want us to do about them, Ray?" one of the men asked. "I don't know if we brought a shovel."

"Hell, check them for anything valuable and take their guns, then leave them for the buzzards. They don't deserve anything else."

Chapter 6

"Julio says as many as six might've gotten away," Clay said as he nudged Loco closer to Ray's bay gelding. The morning sun cast a red glow as it peeked over the horizon.

"Possible. There was a lot of smoke, dust and shooting going on. Anything's possible."

"Ya don't plan on going after them?"

Ray glanced at Clay before shaking his head and guiding the bay around a clump of cactus.

"No, my jurisdiction ends near the Sawyer place. We were stretching it when we chased those devils last night. Besides, I've got a dead member of the posse and Roberta to take care of. I'm heading back to town."

"Well, I don't reckon the U.S. Marshal will cry none about us killing those cutthroats last night," Clay said with a snort. "It sticks in my craw to be letting some of them get away, especially after doing what they did to Roberta."

"It does me too, Clay," Ray growled. "Hell, what they did to George and Martha is enough to make the Lord himself cuss. I'd like nothing better than to string them all up and let them dry like jerky in the sun, but I can't. Ain't nothing stopping you from going after them, if it bothers you that much."

"I might just do that." Clay nudged Loco over a rise as the remains of the Sawyer ranch came into view. "You don't mind if I take Julio with me, do you? I know you had him locked up on a count of a pack of lies Luke Warren told."

"Na, take him," Ray said with a chuckle. "It might stop him from killing Luke next time he sees him."

"Much obliged." Clay turned Loco off the trail and motioned for Teresa and Julio to join him.

"Are you really going to let Clay and his wife go after those guys?" Jess Walker asked. "There's six of them, and only two with Clay, even if he talks Julio into going.

"Julio will go," Ray said. "He ain't got nothing else to do, and he's pretty upset about what happened to Roberta for some reason. I think he'd like to even the score. Besides," Ray chuckled and shook his head, "I'd say those highbinders are a little out-gunned, having to face Clay and Teresa, not counting Julio. I'd like to be there when they catch up with them."

Chapter 7

"It don't make sense." Clay brought Loco to a halt around mid-morning and pushed his hat to the back of his head.

"*¿Qué?*" Teresa stopped tugged on the reins as Diablo sidestepped.

"It looks like they're heading straight toward Eagle Pass, and they ain't even trying to hide their trail. What do you think, Julio?"

"Maybe they think no one is following." The vaquero shrugged as he rolled a cigarette.

"They might be thinking that, or maybe they're thinking of crossing the border. There's a good river crossing there."

"Yes, that is what they are thinking," Teresa said with a nod. "The mules will bring a good price at the mines in Mexico."

"You're both probably right. But we ain't pushing no mules and moving fast, so we should catch them before they cross the river. If not," he shrugged, "there's nothing stopping us from killing them in Mexico." He spurred Loco into a lope.

~ ~ ~

They rode into Eagle Pass late the following day, hot, tired and dusty. The evening breeze was tainted with the scent of water coming from the Rio Grande, making the horses bob their heads and protest their discomfort.

"We'd best tend to the horses before we wind up walking," Clay said and turned Loco toward the livery stables.

The city had grown to a teeming population of over 2,000, and was known for its violence. Large coal deposits had been discovered on the opposite bank of the Rio Grande, and Piedras Negras sprang to life in 1850. It soon became a haven for fugitive slaves. Both banks of the river were infested with outlaws, killers and thieves. In 1855 James H. Callahan made a gallant, but vain, effort to curb some of the violence when he led three companies of volunteers across the river in pursuit of renegade Lipans and Kicakapoos. The Mexican government took exception to the gesture, and Callahan soon found himself in a battle against Mexican forces. He fell back and set the village of Piedras Negras on fire before crossing back into Eagle Pass.

Following the Civil War, bands of cattle thieves and fugitives led by John King Fisher dominated Eagle Pass. It took the aid of the Texas Rangers and the coming of the railroad in 1884, linking Eagle Pass to Galveston and San Antonio, to eventually establish some type of law and order. By then John Fisher had gone from being an outlaw to a legitimate rancher, and even a lawman.

The sight of a pretty Mexican woman brought stares from a seedy looking group loitering in front of the La Hermosa Cantina.

Clay slipped the elderly Mexican who was manning the livery three dollars as Teresa and Julio unsaddled and rubbed down their mounts. Clay had just finished feeding Loco when Julio called from the far end of the livery.

"*Señor* Clay, come look." He pointed toward the animals inside the corral as Clay and Teresa joined him. "They are the mules the *banditos* took. No?"

"Ya got good eyes and even better horse-sense." Clay slapped the *vaquero* on the back. "Yeah, they're Sawyer's mules alright." He turned and yelled toward the gray-headed stable hand.

"Hey, *hombre*. When did these mules come in?"

"Eh?" The old man ambled forward.

"I said, when did these mules get here?"

"Mmm, maybe *una hora*,' he said with a shrug.

"One hour?" Clay glanced toward Teresa, who nodded.

"Where'd the men go who brung them in?"

Teresa translated as he pointed toward the cantina.

"Figures," Clay said with a snort. He slipped the man an extra dollar and checked the loads in his .45. "Tell him to keep an eye on the mules, and explain that they are stolen. He doesn't need to be a hero, just keep watch. Meanwhile, we'd best check in with the law before we do anything."

The old man said the sheriff's office was on the same street, several buildings past the cantina.

He also said the men they were looking for would be easy to find. One of them was a big man with a red shirt and yellow bandana, while another had his left arm in a sling with a bloody bullet hole in the sleeve.

They wove their way past the saloon as a drunken cowboy rushed outside to vomit in the street. Clay snickered as Teresa mumbled a curse in Spanish. He pushed the door to the office open and stepped inside to see Texas Ranger Curtis Hart seated behind the desk.

"Evening, Clay...Teresa." The ranger laid a telegram on the desk and eyed Julio as he closed the door. "Y'all look a little trail-worn."

"We are. We've been trailing some killin' skunks that murdered a family and stole everything they had."

"This have something to do with the Sawyers over near Carrizo Springs?"

"Yeah, same bunch."

"Just been reading about that." He gave the telegram a nudge with his finger across the desk, then pointed toward the coffee pot. "Help yourself, Teresa. It's fresh. And if you can find a clean cup or two, pour us all one."

"*Gracias*," Teresa said, and pulled four cups from the shelf.

"Have any luck tracking your killers?" Curtis asked, as Teresa handed him a steaming mug.

"Yeah. According to the old man at the livery, they entered the cantina about an hour before we rode in."

"They're probably still there. Drink your coffee and we'll go fetch 'em and lock 'em up."

"No offense, but don't you think we ought to check in with the sheriff before we do anything?"

"You can if you want. He's buried out there on the hill, next to the last two they had. Too bad about Hank, though." The ranger shook his head. "He was a nice young man figuring on getting married and raising a family."

"Where's the highbinder that killed him?" Clay asked.

"I rode in a few hours after Hank bought it, and found them at The Long Horn. There were two of them. They argued some when I told them they were under arrest. The difference was, they'd shot Hank in the back, but I was facing them. They're buried on the same hill."

"Good for you." Clay set his mug on the desk. "Ready to go?"

"Might as well." Curtis grabbed his hat and buckled on his gun belt. "By the way. How many are we talking about?"

"Might be as many as six. Is there a problem with that?"

"No, I just like to know what I'm going up against." He grabbed a double-barreled shotgun from the shelf and checked the loads, then paused to stare at Julio.

"He is on our side, isn't he?"

"Yeah," Clay nodded. "That's Julio Garcia, and he's riding with us."

"I know who he is. That's why I asked. Well, let's go get it done."

Chapter 8

They paused and peeked over the batwing doors. Several men on the sidewalk eyed the shotgun in Hart's hand and hurried to the opposite side of the street.

"I think that's them sitting in the middle of the room," Clay said. "The old man at the livery said the men we're looking for would be easy to find. One of them's a big man with a red shirt and yellow bandana, and another has his left arm in a sling with a bloody bullet hole in the sleeve."

"Can't get a better description than that," Hart said. "Ready?"

Julio entered first and worked his way to the bar, elbowing the men on either side.

"Hey, watch it! You made me spill my drink," growled the man on his right. Julio motioned toward the door with his head as Hart entered, carrying the shotgun tucked in the crook of his arm. He was followed closely by Clay and Teresa. Both had already drawn their guns. Teresa stopped about halfway between Julio and Ranger Hart as he approached the table. Clay stopped several steps to the ranger's right.

"Aw, hell!" the man said, downing his whisky in one gulp. "Let's get out of here, Jake." He grabbed his friend by the arm and rushed toward the door. This started a mass exodus with a clatter of chairs as Curtis Hart surveyed the six trail-worn men seated at the table.

"What's all the hardware for? You expecting trouble?" asked the man in the red shirt with a lazy drawl.

"I hear you're the men who brought in those mules over at the livery."

"Yeah? What of it? Is there a law against it?"

"No, but those animals were stolen. Where'd you get 'em?"

"Stolen? Says who?"

"The name's Texas Ranger Curtis Hart. This is Clay Best. The woman beside me is his wife, and the vaquero at the bar is Julio Garcia. Now that we're all acquainted, I'll ask the question once more nice-like, and seeing as those animals belonged to a friend of Clay's, who was murdered along with his wife, you'd best have a good answer. Where'd you get the mules?"

"Stolen, you say? Why we bought those mules from a little farm right outside of town. We didn't know they were stolen. I've got the sales slip right here in my pocket." He reached his hand under the table, but froze as Curtis cocked and pointed the shotgun at his head.

"He lies," Teresa said. "I see this one before. He carries my bullet in his arm."

"You bitch!" The wounded man leaped from the table grabbing for a gun. Teresa shot twice, spinning him off his feet. Clay pulled the trigger as the man closest to him pulled his gun. The blast from Ranger Hart's shotgun killed another. Curtis spun and pulled Teresa to the floor as the remaining two ran toward the door firing. Julio knelt and fired, killing them both. Clay waited for the cloud of smoke to rise then grinned as the vaquero leaned casually against the bar sipping a glass of whiskey.

Teresa came from the floor mumbling in Spanish.

"My, such words coming from a lady," the ranger scolded.

"Why did you pull me to the floor? I could have shot one of them."

"Well, I reckon you did shoot one. Besides, there was so much smoke, I could barely see you, standing not three feet away. I was trying to save your hide."

"Anyway," Clay chuckled, "we had to save a couple for Julio, didn't we?"

She glared at her husband and holstered the gun, then joined Julio at the bar and ordered tequila.

"Huh, I'll bet you don't get any loving tonight," Curtis said as a few patrons carefully slipped inside to view the bodies. "Come on," he slapped Clay on the shoulder, "a drink does sound good about now."

Chapter 9

"I had a sister."

Clay stopped unrolling his bedroll and looked up at Julio. He was sitting on a saddle blanket with his back against a bale of hay, sipping on a bottle of tequila. They had chosen to sleep in the stable in order to keep an eye on their horses and Sawyer's mules.

"What happened to her?" Clay asked as he spread his blankets next to Teresa's, who was tugging on her boots.

"I was in the bean field with our father when men came to the casa. There were five of them. They beat my mother and kicked her in the head. We heard their screams and ran toward the casa, but we had nothing to fight with except our hoes. They shot both me and my father. They thought they had killed me, but the bullet only knocked me out." He parted his hair to show a ragged scar near his right ear. "When I woke, my father was dead and Angela was gone."

"That was your sister's name?" Teresa asked.

"*Si,*" he said with a nod. "They took her. She was fourteen. My mother described the men before she died. I buried her next to my father, then borrowed a gun and followed the men. I found Angela two days later. She was dead too. She had no clothes, so I wrapped her in a blanket and took her home. She is buried next to my mother." He took another swig from the bottle and passed it to Teresa. She crossed herself in prayer and passed the bottle to Clay without taking a sip.

"Did you find them?" Clay asked.

"All but one. He is a big man with no left ear and a patch over his eye. I'll find him some day," Julio said with a nod.

"The others dead?"

Julio nodded.

"Good," Clay toasted the *vaquero* with the bottle. "May they burn in hell."

~   ~   ~

Clay woke before daybreak with his stomach growling. He tugged on his boots, strapped on his gun belt and grabbed his hat, then paused at the door to survey the dusty street. It was empty except for two dogs sniffing at the hitching rail in front of the saloon and a drunk sleeping on the walkway. A light shone in the window of a small restaurant across the street, and Clay patted Antonio on the head with an order to stay before crossing the street. He returned minutes later with a basket of hot tortillas filled with eggs and beans. He tossed one to the dog before setting the basket on a bale of hay. Julio had his horse saddled and was in the process of securing his bedroll.

"Best sit yourself down and grab one of the tortillas before the dog eats them all," Clay said.

"*Gracias*," he said, giving the leather thongs a final tug.

Teresa smiled and motioned for Clay to come closer, then sat upright and kissed him.

"*Buenos días, mi amor*. The basket smells good."

"Better grab what you want. Antonio just finished his, and has his eye on the rest. I couldn't carry three mugs of coffee, so we'll have to drink from the canteens and grab a mug when we return the basket."

"*Bueno*," she said, taking a tortilla and passing the basket to Julio.

Clay waited until they were almost finished before tossing the bottle of tequila to Julio.

"Never thought to ask, but what are your plans, now that we've taken care of Sawyer's killers."

"*No es importante*," he said with a shrug. "Maybe look for the man with one ear."

"How would you feel about ambling along with me and Teresa? We're taking Sawyer's mules and heading into Mexico. We could use someone who's handy with a gun. Might be worth the ride."

Julio studied Clay silently before turning toward Teresa.

"What my husband is trying to say is, we are going after the gold my first husband, Refugio, buried before the Comanches killed him."

"Gold?" Julio took a swig from the bottle and tossed it back to Clay. "How much gold?"

"Better let Teresa tell you about it," Clay said.

"It will be dangerous," she said. "Before the Comanches killed Refugio, he is in charge of a regiment of General Bernal's revolutionaries. They robbed a Federal train that is carrying payroll, and it has much gold. Refugio and his men take all the gold. My Refugio, he hided the gold in a cave by a waterfall near an old hacienda in Mexico. He tells me where it is in case something happens, so I can tell General Bernal. But General Bernal never comes so I can tell him where the gold is hided." Teresa shrugged her shoulders. "Three men came, saying the general sent them, but I did not trust them. I never know why the general doesn't come."

"And no one else knows where the gold is?" Julio reached for the bottle without taking his eyes off Teresa.

"There were three revolutionaries with Refugio when they hided the gold, and those three died when the Comanches killed Refugio, so they cannot get the gold. *Señor* Clay and I think the gold is still there."

"How much gold?"

Teresa shrugged her shoulders. "Refugio said it took a wagon to carry the gold, and it will be dangerous. There are the Federales who wish to have the gold back. Then there are the Comanche and Mescalero Apache. There is also the Yaqui. We will have to be very careful."

Julio grabbed another tortilla and chewed thoughtfully. "Do you know where this place is?"

"*Si*, I was born in the hacienda. It belonged to my mother and father, and they were there when the Comanches killed them. My mother's little sister and I were playing by the waterfall when the Comanches come, and she hid with me inside the cave. The Comanches do not see us, but my mother and father are working in the bean field, and they die. They burned the hacienda and my aunt's father sees the smoke and comes to help, but it is too late. The Comanches are gone. He takes me to my grandmother in Carrizo Springs and tells her what happened and she tells me when I am older. I visit my uncle once, and he showed where I was born, and where my mama and papa are buried. Nobody goes there now because it is dangerous. My uncle is afraid and moves his family to Mexico City. Indians water their horses in the creek, but they never go into the cave because it makes noise in the wind. They say it has a bad spirit, and that's why it is hid behind the waterfall. I showed Refugio where my aunt hid with me, and that is where he hid the gold. I think it is still there."

Julio stared into the distance as he finished the tortilla, then reached for the bottle of tequila.

Clay lit his pipe and took several puffs. "Teresa and me think it would be best to take the mules and pack out what we can carry and leave the rest for later. How does an equal split sound? We all get one third."

"*Si*," Julio said with a nod. We would also need plenty of water and food. When we have the gold, we will need to stay away from the villages until we cross the border. We will also need extra guns and bullets."

"Then we all go?" Teresa asked, letting her eyes bounce between Clay and Julio.

"Yes, I reckon it means we're all going." Clay stood and stretched his long legs. "But like Julio says, we'll need to spend the rest of the day packing the mules. We'd best do it quietly, and not attract attention. Folks can get mighty curious, especially when they see you loading mules with picks, shovels, guns and grub. We don't want any extra company unless we invite them personally."

~   ~   ~

Manuel Rosales leaned in the shadows against the shabby building to watch the line of mules and riders as they passed. They moved quietly, and turned toward the river crossing. Manuel checked the horizon, and guessed it was still an hour before daybreak. El Burro Salvaje was close enough to the Rio Grande for him to see the foam the hooves created as they entered the river. The big yellow dog barked several times before jumping into the water. Manuel had happened to see Teresa the previous morning, and had followed quietly as she spent the day slipping from one store to another with the men. Then she returned to the stable, carrying water bags, food and even two shotguns. The tall gringo had a pick and a shovel tied to the mule he was leading. They might have gotten away unnoticed, except for the fact that Manuel had felt the need to relieve himself. He was returning from the outhouse when he heard the stable doors creak open. The building stood approximately 100 yards from El Burro Salvaje, but the cry of the rusty hinges carried clearly in the quiet morning air. Manuel took a last look at the cigar butt in his fingers before tossing it into the street. He poked his head over the batwing doors and yelled.

"Hey, Miguel, come here."

The grimy revolutionary made his way to the doors rubbing a gnarled hand across his unshaven face. *¿Sí, qué quiere?*

"What do I want? I want you to sober up and look at the woman on the red horse." He grabbed Miguel's hair and pointed toward Teresa. "She's the one I've been telling you about. Isn't that Refugio's woman?"

"*Si*....maybe. I don't know, amigo. It's hard to tell, looking at the back of her head. It could be Teresa. What is she doing with the gringo and Julio Garcia?"

"So, that is Julio?"

"You didn't know it was Julio?"

"No, I've only seen Julio once from a distance, and it was dark."

They watched until the riders had crossed the Rio Grande and disappeared into Piedras Negras.

"Where do you think they are going with the mules?" Miguel asked.

"I'll tell you where I think they are going, *amigo*. I think they are going after the gold Refugio stole from the *Federales*"

"Gold?"

"Si, gold," Manuel said with a nod. "Remember when we rode with General Bernal, and he had us rob a Federale train with a wagonload of gold?"

"*Si.*"

"Bernal sent Refugio and three men to hide the gold while we attracted a small regiment of Federales. Refugio and his men never returned. Bernal sent me, Romero and Juan to his woman's *jacale* in Carrizo Springs to find out where they were. His woman said the Comanches had killed them all in a raid on Carrizo Springs, and showed us their graves. Bernal thought the gold was lost. But I think Refugio told his woman where he hid it. Now, I think they are going to get it.

"Come," he slapped Miguel on the back. "Let's get the others and follow. If they know where the gold is, we will wait until they have it, then take what belongs to us."

Chapter 10

Clay stopped midday and mopped his forehead with his bandana, before wiping the sweatband in his hat. Then he tied the bandana around his neck, and shaded his eyes with the hat as he glanced at the sun.

"Best make camp here for a couple of hours and rest the animals. Julio, help me stake them by that clump of mesquite, then slip off into the bushes like you're gonna take a pee. Circle back to that little rise and see if you can figure out who our company is."

"We're being followed?" Teresa's voice was dry and raspy.

"Yeah, I noticed them about two hours ago when Antonio was acting funny. You'd better start nursing that canteen. I don't want you drying up in this heat and blowing away."

"They may not mean anything," Julio said, loosening the cinches on his saddle. "They could be taking the same trail, but going somewhere different."

"Could be, but it ain't likely." Clay tied one of the pack mules to the mesquite and grinned. "They're hanging back and traveling at the same pace as us. I'd say we've picked up some company, and I'd like to know how many, and who they are."

"*Si,*" Julio said with a nod, as he disappeared into the brush.

Teresa dug a small pack of jerky from one of the saddle bags and handed a piece to Clay. They sat on a sandy mound in the shade and chewed in silence, listening to the munching of the mules and horses as they nibbled at the mesquite.

"Think they mean trouble?" Teresa asked after a minute.

Clay took a sip from the canteen. "Whoever it is most likely saw the pack animals and figured we're prospecting; decided they'd follow and see what we've found. Even if we came up empty-handed, our horses, mules and supplies would bring a hefty price."

They both grabbed for their guns and turned as Julio rustled back through the brush. Clay relaxed and passed the canteen.

"Were you able to get a good look?"

"*Si,*" he said with a nod, then took a sip. "Four men, and I think they are following. I recognized one as being Manuel Rosales."

Clay glanced at Teresa as she swore in Spanish.

"Ya'll act as though you know the *hombre.*"

"He was one of Bernal's men. He was always trying to put his hands on me when Refugio was not around. I swore I'd kill him if he tried it again. He just laughed. I did not trust him then, and I do not trust him now."

"Well, this just gets more interesting by the minute." Clay handed Julio a couple of hunks of jerky before fishing a second for himself.

"Want me to go back and kill them?" Julio asked.

"No, not yet. We're down here now, and it's best we keep quiet. I don't want to attract any soldiers and have them ask what we're doing, or why we killed four men."

"You will have to kill Manuel anyway," Teresa snapped.

"Probably, but let's do it farther away than a half a day's ride from the border."

~　　　~　　　~

They spent the first night in Fuente, and were packed and on the move before daylight. Early afternoon on the third day, when they stopped on a rise over-looking the small village, Clay pushed his hat to the back of his head and stared. The focal point seemed to be a large make-shift cantina sporting walls made of adobe bricks and a roof consisting of weathered boards and canvas. Several *jacales* were scattered about haphazardly, and a corral stood about fifty yards from the cantina. Crude painted letters on the side of a rambling one-story adobe boasted of being the restaurant and boarding house. The condition of the church gave Clay the impression that the building had not been used in years. A small trickle of a creek snaked its way through the middle of town and past a shed where a hog was being butchered.

"What in God's name is this burg," Clay asked.

"*Santa Inez*," Teresa said somberly.

"I don't recall ever hearing about it, or seeing it on a map," Clay said.

"You won't," Julio said. "It doesn't really exist. A nun named Inez came here with several sisters from her convent and built the chapel, hoping to evangelize the Indians. She got sick with fever and died. The bishop called the remaining sisters back to the convent. Then some of Bernal's men started using the church as a hideout. Later, someone built the cantina and the *palacio residencia*, then more started coming. They are all bad. Don't trust any of them, *Señor* Clay."

"I hadn't planned on doing that. They got some sort of dry-goods store here?"

"*Sí*." Julio pointed toward a large rambling building toward the end of town. "The *Almacén General*. They steal from farmers and supply wagons, then sell it for a huge profit."

"Figures. Well, let's just mosey down and see if we can't water and feed the animals, and maybe grab a bite to eat," Clay said, and nudged his horse forward. "I hate to buy stolen goods, and since we don't really need supplies, we'll just bypass the store. If we think it's safe enough, we might unload our grip and spend the night."

"*Si*, I need a bath badly, Teresa said.

"I reckon we all do." Clay chuckled.

The man in charge of the stable was a one-eyed, middle-aged stable hand, sporting an ugly scar across his missing eye and down his left cheek.

"The mules and horses had best be here, and all our belongings intact when we get back, or I'll blow your brains out. Got that?" Clay growled.

"*Si*," the man said with a vigorous nod, glancing toward Antonio as the dog growled. Julio handed him several silver coins and swatted his shoulder. They were slipping the packs off the mules when the door to the cantina flew open. A young girl dashed toward the corral and past Clay and Teresa to hide behind Julio. She poked her head around his side and stared wide-eyed toward the cantina. The door swung open again as a huge shaggy man ran out.

"Where is she? Where is that little bitch?" he yelled.

One of the men pointed, and he half ran and half stumbled across the wide street. He paused, seeing the girl, who was still peeking around Julio, and ran his fingers down several raw scratches on his right cheek.

"There you are." He grabbed for her hair, but she ducked behind Julio.

"Don't let him get me. Please help me," the girl said in Spanish.

Teresa stepped between the man and Julio. "What is this about?"

"None of your damned business." He grabbed for the girl again, but stopped when Teresa drew one of her pistols and jammed it against his ear.

"Now, I ask once more," she said, cocking the hammer. "What is this about?" Clay slowly drew his Colt and cocked the hammer, holding it against his leg, as several others gathered outside the stable to watch.

"What's it about? She's mine! I bought and paid for her," he bellowed. "I gave her father fifty dollars for her."

"She is a young girl, not a horse or a dog," Teresa yelled.

"Hell, what are you, some kind of nun?" He laughed. "It happens all the time." I gave her paw some money, and she's mine! Now, get the hell out of my way."

"Cilatocas tebol adar un balaso en los guebos." Teresa spoke in a low voice.

Julio and the crowd gathered at the stable all burst into laughter as the man stepped backward and glanced around.

"In case you did not *comprender señor*, she says if you touch the *chica*, she will shoot your balls off. Then, I will have to kill you."

"You'd best listen to them, if you know what's good for you, mister," Clay said. "They mean what they say. You'd have better luck getting your money back from her pa."

"I don't want the money," the man yelled. "I want her."

"Suit yourself," Clay said with a snort. "But you're gonna wind up dead."

"Okay," the man roared. "I can't fight all of you by myself. But this ain't over. I'll be back, and bring some help."

Clay waited until the man had crossed the street and entered the cantina before holstering his gun. He heaved a deep sigh and glared toward Julio, as the vaquero pulled the saddle from his horse.

"Better re-saddle that mustang, son. I think we just wore out what welcome we had." He motioned toward the cantina where a crowd was still gathered, all watching the corral. Julio stared for a few seconds before shrugging and tossing the lather-soaked blanket and saddle back on the horse.

"You'd best consider what she's gonna ride, 'cause you can't leave her here, and she ain't riding behind me," Clay said as he tightened the cinches on Loco. "Now, don't go looking at me to solve your problem." He laughed as Julio stared. "She ran to you, and you and Teresa stood up for her. She's your problem, not mine."

"You wouldn't leave her," Teresa snapped.

"Didn't say I would." He led Loco and one of the mules out of the corral. "But the fact is, we've got enough trouble with several men following us, and looking out for Indians, without taking on some teenage Indian girl to boot." He laughed as Julio turned to study the girl.

"Don't tell me you didn't notice she was Indian? The only question is, what tribe. I just hope she ain't stolen, and her folks aren't out looking for her."

~ ~ ~

They stopped several miles southeast of town and made camp by the creek. Clay shoveled sand and gravel from the creek bed, making a small reservoir for the animals to drink from. Teresa made coffee and tortillas, and heated a can of beans over the campfire. They sat in a circle around the fire, eating in silence. Clay finished his coffee and was fixing to pour a second cup when he burst out laughing.

"What is so funny?" Teresa asked.

"Well," he said, warming her cup, "I've neutered a few head of cattle in my time, and gelded a few horses, but I ain't never done it with a .38 Smith and Wesson."

"I was angry. He was molesting this child. I know how it feels to be treated that way."

"I ain't blaming you none. Don't forget, I knocked Hugh Tullis on his backside when I found out he was the one that hurt you. I was close to killing him when Ray stopped me."

"*Sí*, I know that." She nodded.

"I just thought it was funny...that's all." Clay stopped to study the young girl."

"Do you speak and understand any English?"

"*Sí*, a little."

"That's good." He leaned back against his saddle and sipped the coffee. "What's your name?" The girl stared at him blankly before Teresa took over.

"*¿Cómo te llamas?*"

"Estrella," the girl said with a shrug.

"That's a pretty name," Clay said. "Did your pa really sell you to that man?" He had to wait for Teresa to translate.

"She says no," Teresa said at last. Her parents are dead. She was kidnapped from her village, and sold as a slave. The woman who bought her got jealous because of her husband and sold her to that man this afternoon."

"Figures," Clay said quietly. He studied the girl over the rim of his tin cup. He set it aside as she shivered. "Reckon we'd best get her some clothes next chance we get. It's October, and the weather's fixing to turn. Here," he said, pulling an old leather jacket from his saddlebag. He slipped it around her shoulders. "It don't look like much, but it'll keep you from freezing in that thin dress you've got on."

He sat back down as the other three grinned.

"What?"

"You act so mean and gruff, but you're a puppy like Antonio," Teresa said with a laugh.

"Huh." Clay snorted. "I've been called the offspring of a dog before, but never a puppy. Besides, Antonio's hardly a puppy. Reckon I could be in worse company than him. Ain't that right, boy," he said, ruffling the dog's ears.

~   ~   ~

"I know it's her, Leo." He studied the shabby looking man in peasant clothing. Leo Santiago had ridden into Santa Inez with Manuel Rosales and Miguel Villa about a half an hour earlier, but headed toward the cantina, while Manuel questioned the old man at the stable. Leo refilled the man's glass with tequila.

"Go on. How do you know it's Teresa Romero?

The peasant took a sip of tequila and leaned across the table. "She rides Refugio's horse, Diablo. She had two hombres with her. A big Americano, and a pistolero I have seen some place before.

"*Sí*," he said with a nod. "The big gringo is named Clay Best. He used to be the marshal at Cool Water, across the border in Texas."

Leo took his time refilling their glasses. He disagreed with Manuel's heavy-handed tactics of beating information out of someone. He believed you could get more reliable information quicker by supplying a few drinks to the right people. It hadn't taken Leo but a few minutes before spotting Pedro. Pedro Nunez had ridden in Bernal's band of revolutionaries, but he was now a hopeless drunk.

"I heard the other man is Julio Garcia. Is that true?"

"I've only seen Julio once, and that was over a year ago." Pedro scratched his chin and took another sip of tequila. "Come to think of it, he could be Julio; he's the right age."

"That's okay, my friend. Are they still here in Santa Inez?"

"No, no..." he said shaking his head. "They left about an hour ago with the girl."

"Girl? What girl?" Leo asked.

"I don't know her name. She was a young Indian slave. The fat gringo called Wade bought her, but they took her."

Leo stared at the sloppy red-faced man at the bar. His clothes were dirty and sweat-stained, and he looked like he hadn't bathed in a month.

"Why did they take her?" Leo motioned toward the bartender for another bottle of tequila.

"The girl doesn't like Wade and scratched his face. Then she runs out of the cantina and to the corral, where she hides behind Julio Garcia. The fat gringo goes after her, but Teresa points a gun in his ear and threatens to shoot him if he touches the *chica* again."

Leo laughed as he poured more tequila.

"It sounds like her. Remember when she shot Pablo's sombrero off his head when he patted her behind? I think she would have killed him, if Refugio had not stopped her. Can you tell me which way they went when they left Santa Inez?"

"*Sí*," Pedro said with a nod. "They go that way, to the southwest." He pointed.

"Bueno." He poured more tequila. "I tell you what, my friend," he swatted Pedro on the shoulder as Manuel and Miguel entered the cantina, "how would you like to ride with us? It could prove quite profitable for us all."

"Profitable? How?"

"Profitable in gold, my friend. Very profitable," Leo said in a whisper, then put a finger to his lips as he motioned toward the crowded bar with his head.

"*Sí*," Pedro said with a slow nod. "I would like that very much."

"That old idiot at the stables could tell us nothing," Manuel said loudly as he and Miguel pulled chairs to the table.

"Maybe not, but my friend Pedro can. We've been talking, and we know that the woman is Teresa Romero, and the old gringo with her is Clay Best. We also know the young vaquero is Julio Garcia, and they took the Indian girl. But mostly," he paused to pour tequila, "Pedro knows which way they went. And as soon as we finish our tequila, he is going to help us find them.

Chapter 11

They arrived in Nava late the following day, and worked out a plan where one of them was always with Estrella for her safety. She told them her last name was Moreno, and that she was sixteen years old, although Clay figured she looked like she was twelve. She also told them the man who had stolen her from her village had sold her before, several times, but she ran away each time. She said he never seemed to mind, since that meant he could sell her again, making even more money. The man she was sold to this time was different. He was offensive, and frightened her. She refused to go with him.

They went about getting extra supplies and baths, before grabbing a bite to eat. Teresa had taken the precaution of ordering Antonio to stay close to Estrella. Clay snickered as the first man they approached jumped from the walkway when the dog snarled.

"I reckon she's safe enough for now." He paused and surveyed the street. taking his time to pack tobacco in his pipe, he dug a match from his pocket.

"Don't let on that we notice him, but do you see the fella leaning against the corner of the cantina in the shade?"

"*Sí*," Julio said. "He was one of them watching us at Santa Inez."

"I thought so. Maybe we'd better not spend the night here. It might be best to make camp somewhere down the road, where we can keep an eye on our grip and each other."

"*Bueno.*" Teresa nodded and took Estrella by the arm. "We go."

"I reckon it wouldn't hurt to fill our water bags and canteens at the fountain. When we hit open country again, we just might drop back and make acquaintances with our company. It wouldn't hurt none to know who we are traveling with."

~   ~   ~

The sun was beginning to set when they found the stream at the base of a small canyon, just wide enough for one horse and rider at a time. The pack mules were able to squeeze through by wading midstream. The canyon finally widened to a small grassy area with several trees, where the cool water gushed from a split in the rocks at the base of a wall that loomed thirty feet above their heads.

"Huh, we rode ourselves into a box canyon," Clay said, sliding from the saddle. "Ain't much of a way to escape if you're attacked."

"There's no place to attack, except the way we came," Teresa said.

Clay held out his arms to help her down. "They could always shoot at us from the rocks above."

"*Carumba*, you always look at the bad side. We can always shoot back, if they do."

Clay laughed and kissed her forehead. "I know we can, and I was only pointing out the possibilities."

"You think they'll try robbing us here?" Julio asked.

"Na, not unless it's the fat man who claims to own her." Clay gestured toward Estrella. "They ain't stupid enough to try riding upstream single file, knowing we'll pick 'em off one at a time. They'll wait until we leave and are in the open. My guess is at least one or two of them know what we're after, and will wait until we have it. Then they'll come with a vengeance."

"Then, what do we do?" Teresa pulled the saddle from Diablo and laid it at the base of a small cottonwood.

"Well, first question is, how far is it to your pa's old farm and the cave?"

Teresa wrinkled her eyebrows and shook her head.

"Maybe two days. Rufugio said it was forty miles south of Carrizo Springs."

"That's what I was hoping. We'll hole up here and rest the animals for a couple of days. Once we get the gold loaded on the mules, we'll be crossing open desert, and trying to out-run that band of cutthroats."

"Bueno," Julio said with a nod, unsaddling his horse. He motioned toward Estrella and spoke softly in Spanish. The girl ran to unpack one of the mules.

Clay and Julio scoured the small wooded area for fallen tree branches and dry wood. Estrella filled a bucket with water, then placed rocks for a campfire as Clay and Julio set up two small tents. Clay was unrolling his and Teresa's bedrolls when Julio took one of the shotguns and walked back downstream. Several minutes later, two blasts from the shotgun rang out.

Clay jumped to his feet and grabbed his Winchester. He rounded the bend, stumbling over a large rock and skinning his knuckles. He cursed and slipped on another stone, almost falling into the stream. He jumped back to his feet as Teresa joined his side with both pistols drawn.

"My hell, boy. You liked to have scared us to death," he growled as Julio appeared carrying two sage hens. "Next time, tell us when you're going hunting."

"Bueno," Julio said with a shrug. "I did not think you would mind."

"I don't mind about the birds. Just tell me first."

~   ~   ~

Teresa and Estrella chatted merrily as they prepared supper, and surprised the men with a version of chicken mole, made from the sage hens and powdered chocolate

Teresa had been carring in her pack. They served the meal with tortillas and a bottle of red wine.

Clay was feeling relaxed as he got ready for bed. He and Teresa had one tent, while Estrella took the other. Julio made his bedroll close to Estrella's tent as Antonio trotted into camp, looking satisfied with himself. The dog stretched and yawned, then found a comfortable spot between the tents.

Clay crawled out of his tent at daybreak to check on the animals. He found the mules and horses exactly as they had left them the night before. There had been little chance they would wander too far from the fresh grass and water.

He returned to the campsite to find Teresa standing in front of their tent, staring at Julio's bedroll. He didn't see what she was seeing at first, then chuckled as he gave the vaquero a nudge with his boot.

"Get cold in the middle of the night?"

Julio opened his eyes, then sat up quickly as he realized Estrella was snuggled next to him.

"Santa Maria, Dios! What are you doing in my bed, woman?"

Estrella yawned and stretched before smiling. "I was cold and frightened that man would come in the middle of the night. So, I joined you."

"There's little chance anyone's gonna sneak up on us at night, with Antonio around," Clay said. "I'm gonna get some firewood and let's get the coffee going. Then we'll discuss the rest of the day."

After breakfast, the women washed clothes in the stream and bathed, while Julio took the shotgun and disappeared through the trees with an announcement that he was going hunting. Clay took Antonio and scouted the surrounding area, looking for a second way out of the canyon. About midday he found what he was looking for. It was a seldom-used trail hidden behind a thick cottenwood grove. It climbed steeply up the side of the canyon. Clay's lungs burned when he reached the top, but he felt like he could see forever. From his vantage point, he not only could see their own campsite, but he could see a second camp downstream.

Climbing back down, he worked his way downstream. He quieted the dog as a low rumble begged to build in his throat. Climbing over several large boulders, he took a position behind a clump of greasewood. Not fifty yards ahead were their followers, huddled around a small campfire. Clay climbed carefully down and patted the dog.

"Come on, boy," he whispered. "I think we've found what we were looking for."

He was close to their camp when he spotted Julio, hidden behind a clump of brush, watching the camp. Clay approached quietly. Julio glanced at him, then went back to watching.

"Anything wrong?" he whispered, placing a hand on the vaquero's shoulder.

"*Sí*," he whispered. "I think she was a little chica, like my sister. But she is not a child, *Señor* Clay."

Clay peered through the brush to see Estrella bathing in the creek. While the girl was a tiny little thing in Clay's opinion, her body curved in the right places like a grown woman.

"I'll say. What'd you expect? She said she was sixteen." Clay glanced toward the bank to see Teresa, wrapped in a towel, combing her long black hair.

"What the hell are you spying on them for while they're taking a bath?" Clay almost shouted as he swatted Julio's shoulder. "You were watching my wife?

"No, no, no, *Señor* Clay." He held up both hands in defense. "*Señora* Best, she was finished when I looked. I swear."

Excited female voices caught their attention. Estrella was out of the water wrapping a towel around her body as both women ran toward the tents. Antonio barked and bolted after the women as Clay straightened to tower over Julio and wave a finger in his face.

"Boy, I catch you spying on my wife while she's bathing, and I'll shoot your eyes out." He turned and walked quickly toward camp, ignoring Julio's pleas.

"I swear on my mother's grave, *Señor* Best. I see nothing."

~   ~   ~

The men around the campfire jerked up at the sound of gunfire. First one shot, followed seconds later by a second.

"Shotgun," Leo said. "One of them is hunting again." He had hoped to slip away and join Clay Best before now, but Manuel Rosales had ridden too close, and had made it known that he would shoot the first man that tried to desert. Then, he had watched with a sick feeling in the pit of his stomach as the gang beat and robbed a peasant farmer of what little food he and his pregnant wife had. Leo had washed the trail dust from his body that morning in the cold creek, but he still felt like he needed to bathe. He decided that he'd waited long enough. He would make his move one way or the other that morning.

"Yeah, and they are eating real food, instead of this," Jose Rios said with a scowl and waved a stick of jerky in the air. "I smelled chicken coming from their camp last night, and bacon and coffee this morning. I say we go into their camp, eat their food and make them tell us where the gold is."

"Go right ahead," Miguel said with a laugh. "You are welcome to try. There is only one way into the canyon, and one way out. You'll make a nice target for the old gringo and his rifle."

"He's right," Manuel Rosales said. "They are resting the horses, which means they are close to the gold. They will be on the move again soon, and we will follow. We'll know when they have the gold. Gold is heavy, and the mules will be moving slow. They will have to cross open ground, and that's when we make our move."

"Well, that is fine, if you want to wait, but I am tired and hungry. Juan and I are going back to Santa Inez," one of the men said. The three men had joined them after hearing Manuel's loud voice talking about the gold inside the cantina, and Leo was glad to be rid of them. That would mean three less bandits to contend with. He toasted them with the bottle of brandy and laughed.

"You thought it was going to be easy? It is never easy taking gold from someone, especially when they are Clay Best and Julio Garcia. Go back to the cantina and find a woman to keep you warm."

"That's all I hear from you," Manuel said with a snort. "Who the hell is this Clay Best you're talking about? I saw him once in Carrizo Springs, and he just looked like an old gringo to me."

"Eh? You will soon get acquainted with the real Marshal Best once you try to take the gold." Leo licked the paper on the cigarette he had been rolling. "I worked for Lester Bishop years ago, and Clay Best was the marshal at Cool Water. I saw him kill a man more than once. He might look like an old tired gringo to you, but he's quicker than a snake with his gun, and doesn't mind killing."

"If he's so mean and deadly, then why are you here with the rest of us?" Manuel snorted a second time and laughed.

"Oh, I'm here for the gold, same as the rest of you. But I'm also wondering how long it will take, before he comes down that creek and kills you."

"Maybe I should kill you first." Manuel grabbed for his gun, but stopped when Leo drew and cocked his revolver. He let the pistol drop back into the holster and stared.

"That's better," Leo said with a smile. He chuckled as Jose Rios and the other two rode away without Manuel firing a shot or trying to stop them.

"I'd hate to kill you before I had a chance to watch. But," he holstered his own weapon, "just to show you I hold no grudges, I'll ride upstream to their camp and find out when they plan on moving. After all, the plan is to attack *after* they have the gold. Isn't it?" He grinned and walked toward his horse.

Chapter 12

Clay could hear the horse's iron shoes clacking sharply against rocks long before the rider appeared, working his way upstream. He motioned with his head and Julio patted Estrella on the shoulder. They both disappeared through the brush, clutching rifles. He had no idea if the girl knew how to use the gun, but it would give their visitor pause just seeing her armed. Teresa crossed the campground and sat on a fallen log, holding one of the pistols in her lap. Clay removed his revolver and cocked the hammer as the rider stopped mid-stream and shaded his eyes with his sombrero.

"*Hola*, in the camp. Is it alright if I come visit, *Señor* Clay?"

"Suit yourself, Leo. You coming peaceful-like, or looking to get yourself killed?"

The rider laughed loudly as he urged the horse forward. "Ho, I come like a little mouse, *Señor* Clay. I am no fool." He rode to the edge of the camp and dismounted.

"See," he said as he unbuckled his gun belt and hung it over the saddle horn. He sat on a rock near Clay and grinned. "You may tell Julio and the girl I mean no harm. They may come join us and keep their guns if they like. I've seen you kill too many men to try anything stupid." Leo took a deep breath and exhaled slowly as he surveyed the campground.

"Very nice, you chose well. I heard you got remarried after June died. Is that true?"

"Yes, it is." Clay motioned toward Teresa. "I married Teresa. Teresa, this fellow is Leo Santiago. We rode together for Lester Bishop."

"*Sí*, those were good times, before we discovered he was a coyote." Leo motioned toward the coffee pot.

"The coffee smells good *señora*. May I?"

"*Sí*," Teresa said, holstering her gun. She filled a tin mug and passed it to Leo as Julio and Estrella came from the bushes and sat opposite the visitor, cradling the rifles in their laps. Leo closed his eyes as he sipped from the mug.

"Ah, it has been three days since I tasted coffee."

"They ain't got none in that makeshift camp downstream?" Clay asked.

"No." Leo laughed and shook his head. "They think the gold you are looking for is close, and they didn't bring food or warm clothes. I tried to tell them you are packed for a long trip, but Manuel would not listen."

"Is he the one ramrodding outfit?" Clay asked, refilling Leo's cup.

"*Sí*, he saw you back in Eagle Pass, and thinks because you're leading mules, you are going after the gold *Señora* Best's first husband stole." He studied Clay over the rim of his cup.

"Are they right, *Señor* Clay? Are you looking for gold that Refugio hid?"

Clay snorted and set his cup on the ground, then tapped his fingers against the .44 lying in his lap.

"I figured it might be you with that bunch when I spied your camp yesterday, but I wasn't sure. I knew you as an honest, hard-working cowboy when we worked for Les Bishop. That's why I always chose you when I needed a hand. What happened Leo? Why are you with that bunch of riff raff downstream?"

Leo raised his eyebrows and nodded. "That's a fair question. I may be with them, *Señor* Clay, but I am not with them. When there is no rain, there are no cattle, and no one needs a vaquero. I got married, *Señor* Clay. I have a wife and *niño* who are cold and hungry. I tried working in the mines at Piedras Negras, but the work is dangerous, and the men cough black sickness from their lungs." He shook his head. "That is not for me. If I die, who takes care of my woman and son?

"Then, I heard Manuel talking loudly inside the cantina, telling the others that you are after gold that a man named Refugio stole for Bernal. Then, when I see so many men wanting to follow you and take the gold, I think maybe *Señor* Clay needs help. But," he shook his head laughing, "I forgot how smart *Señor* Clay really is. You sit here, eating good food and drinking coffee, while they are cold and hungry. Already, three of them left this morning to go home. You stay longer and maybe they will all leave."

"That was the idea. I figured if we sat here long enough, they'd either run out of supplies or get tired of waiting." Clay took a sip of coffee and studied the man over the brim of his tin cup. "You went off and left you wife and son alone in that hell-hole of a town?"

"She is with her mother. I left them with all my money, except a few pesos. I told her I was going to look for work. Now, I will stay long enough to see you kill Manuel and Miguel, then I will go to them. Maybe I will find work on the way."

"What makes you think I'm going to kill them?"

"You may not want to kill Manuel Rosales and Miguel Villa, *señor*, but you will have to, or they will kill you."

"He is right," Teresa said as she crinkled her forehead. "They both rode for Bernal with Refugio, but Refugio was not like them. Neither was Leo."

"You two know each other?" Clay's eyes bounced from one to the other.

"*Sí*, I rode a short time with General Bernal, but I did not like it, so I quit and worked for Lester Bishop. It was safer herding cows than robbing *federales*."

"And more honest," Clay said. "Now, what's this about the fellows downstream?"

"Refugio stole, and killed a few *federales*," Teresa said, "but these men kill when there is no reason to kill. They are vicious."

"That is why I come here *Señor* Clay, to tell you. Two days ago, Manuel and Miguel take men in search of food and drink. Instead of buying from a store, they robbed and beat a peasant farmer. I did't see what they did to his woman, but Andren, the young boy with them, told me Manuel and Miguel abused the peasant's young wife after beating her. The woman, she was going to have a baby, but that did not stop them. That is who you are dealing with. Now," he added getting to his feet, "I will leave you."

"Wait." Teresa grabbed several tortillas left from their mid-day meal and filled them with rice and beans, while Estrella rolled them tightly in a scarf.

"You said three men left this morning. How many you figure are still following us?" Clay asked.

"Twelve, maybe thirteen," Leo said with a shrug. "But I think most of them do not wish to fight. Look for Manuel and Miguel, and the fat one who wants the girl. They are the ones to keep an eye on. The rest may run."

"Which side are you going to be on when the shooting starts?" Clay rose to his feet and holstered his pistol.

"I will be on my side, *Señor* Clay. If you ask my help, I will be on yours. If not," he shrugged, "I will wait to see who wins. Maybe you will kill each other and I will have the gold."

"If you fight against us, I'll kill you, Leo. I'd hate to do it, but I would." Clay said.

"I would hate it worse, *Señor* Clay," Leo said with a laugh. "I will not fight against you, I give you my word. But I will not fight for you, unless I am part of your family."

"We're not sure the gold is even still there, Leo. If you're asking for a cut, you might get a cut of nothing."

"You misunderstand me, *señor*. I don't ask for much gold. I only want enough to get my María and son and move where there is work. They go hungry now, and I have nothing to give."

"Sounds fair." Clay nodded.

"Which shall it be, *señor*?"

"Let's think about it. I still don't quite know if I can trust you."

"Bien, *Señor* Clay." He nodded, then grinned as Teresa handed him the scarf filled with tortillas.

"*Gracias, señora.* I shall see you later." Leo touched the brim of his sombrero and leaped into the saddle.

"You know Leo?" Julio asked, as Clay watched the *vaquero* disappear downstream.

"The Leo Santiago I knew was an honest cowboy and one of the few friends I had in Cool Water. I knew he had a shady past and was really fast and accurate with a gun. But he seemed honest, and had a tender spot, especially for women and children. It almost gotten him killed once."

Clay sat on a rock and began packing tobacco into his pipe.

"I enlisted Leo's help tracking down a band of rustlers that had made off with thirty head of Cool Water cattle. Instead of heading south toward the Rio Grande, they took a northwest direction toward Eagle Pass. We figured they planned to sell the cattle across the river at the coal mines in Piedras Negras. They took a wide birth around Carrizo Springs, and were pushing the steers across some rugged country. We caught up with them at Satan's Well, fifteen miles west of Carrizo Springs. That's when the rustlers decided to make a fight, instead of running.

"I told Leo to take his Winchester and make a run toward some rocks, while I covered him. Well, Leo took off, running hunched-over the minute I opened fire. All six rustlers crowded behind some boulders near the opening to Satan's Well, shooting. I squeezed off a shot that caught one of them in the throat. He dropped his rifle and staggered a few steps, then fell.

"Leo quickly dispatched two more, before the rest made a dash for their horses. I was able to drop another as he was swinging into the saddle. One of the men galloped away, leaning in the saddle, with his left arm dangling limp.

"Then Leo made a dash across the open toward the boulders. I was figuring on giving him a good cussing, then I heard a man crying for help. Leo waved, and I ran to where he was crouched.

"I figured it might be a trap, so I told him to be careful, and sent him one way, while I circled the boulder the opposite way.

"We reached the other side of the boulder without finding any rustler. Then we heard him calling for help again. Leo said it was coming from the opening of the chasm. We crept through the rocks and cactus, and found our rustler, clinging to a rock about five feet below the opening. He wasn't nothing but a boy, no more than sixteen or seventeen, and scared to death.

"I told him to hang on, while I fetched a rope. About that time, he wiggled for a better grip and the rock shifted, sending dirt and gravel down the hole.

"Leo yelled there wasn't time, and removed his gun belt. Then, the idgit lay on his stomach, trying to reach the lad, but his arm came about two feet short. He told me to hold his legs, and scooted toward the hole.

"I reminded him there was a rope on a sorrel that one of the rustlers had been riding, but he kept yelling there wasn't enough time. He slid farther into the opening and the boy let go of the rock with his right hand and grabbed Leo's wrist. The extra weight pulled Leo head-first toward the chasm. I grabbed his legs and hauled back, trying to pull them both upward. Then, the load got lighter."

Clay shook his head and took his time lighting the pipe.

"Still makes my blood turn cold, remembering that boy's scream. It took a couple of seconds before we heard him hit bottom, followed by the rattling of hundreds of diamond back rattlesnakes."

Teresa crossed her breast, whispering a prayer.

"Anyway, I hauled Leo out of the hole and fell back, sweating. I told him it was a damned stupid thing to do. He agreed, but said he couldn't let him die."

"Well, I figured he was a knothead, and we had just let him die. I still think we might've saved him, if I had tossed a rope down to him. Instead, Leo almost got pulled in with him."

"Maybe there wasn't time, if the rock was slipping," Teresa said. "And, he was just a boy," she added, shaking her head slowly.

"Yeah, he was at that. But he was also a rustler, and had been shooting at us a few minutes earlier." Clay drew deeply on the pipe.

"Besides," he stood and arched his back. "If we'd saved him, and hauled him back to Carrizo Springs for trial, the judge would've hung him."

Clay stood and jammed his hat down on his head and grinned at Teresa.

"The thing is, that soft spot he's got almost got him killed. That was two years ago, and I don't figure he's changed. Leo quit Cool Water shortly before June passed, and this is the first I've heard from him since. Right now, he's riding with Manuel Rosales and Miguel Villa, and I know what they're capable of. I'm just sorry I didn't kill them both when I had the chance in Carrizo Springs last year."

Clay knocked the ashes from his pipe and went to check on the animals Leo had given him a lot to cogitate on. Maybe the gold wasn't all that important after all, especially when they had thirteen men looking to take it away, and he had Teresa and Estrella to look after.

Chapter 13

They had no more finished breakfast when Teresa dashed into the bushes near the creek and began heaving. Clay set his empty plate aside, stared at Julio and Estrella a couple of seconds, then followed after her.

He found her on her hands a knees, vomiting at the creek's edge.

"You okay?" he asked, placing a gentle hand against her back.

"*Sí*," she said with a nod. He felt her body tense as a second bout of heaving started.

"No, you're not okay." Clay removed his bandana, dipped it in the cool water and wrung it out. "Here," he said, parting her hair and placing the wet cloth against the back of her neck.

"*Gracias*. I'm okay....really I am. I just woke feeling queasy in the stomach, but, I'm okay now."

She washed her face and hands then looked at him and smiled.

"See, I'm all better. Let's enjoy the day."

They returned to the campsite, where Teresa sat on a small boulder, sipping coffee and laughing. A few minutes later, she dashed back to the bushes.

"Lord have mercy," Clay said with a deep sigh. "You two will have to take over most of her chores until she gets over whatever it is ailing her."

"*Sí*," Julio said, nodding toward Teresa. "We will also say prayers for her."

"You do that," Clay said with a firm nod. He again wet and rung out the bandana, placing it against the back of her neck.

"*Perdón, lo siento.* I don't know what is wrong with me," she said, shaking her head.

"No need to apologize to me. I don't reckon it's your fault you ain't feeling good." Clay held her cheeks in his palms to study her face.

"What do you think it is?" she asked.

"I ain't got a clue. Do you hurt anywhere?"

"No. Clay sat on his heels mopping her face the the wet bandana.

"Do you need to heave again?"

"No," she shook her head. "I will be okay." She looked up at Clay and smiled.

"I am sorry to be such a baby. I will do better."

"Well, there ain't nothing to be sorry for. Now, come on." Clay stood and held out his hand for her to take. "Let's go join the others."

******

Clay stuck close to the campsite the rest of the day, cleaning and oiling his guns. By midafternoon, he was satisfied that whatever had been making Teresa sick had passed. She argued with Estrella when the girl insisted on doing most of the work. Then, she growled at Clay and accused him of conspiring with the others to treat her like an invalid.

"I told you I was feeling good!" she yelled.

"Yeah, but you said that earlier, then ran to the creek and heaved your guts out," Clay snapped back.

"But it is gone. See?" She shot her arms upward, then bent over to touch her toes. "I am not sick. You do not have to take care of me."

57

"Okay, I'll leave you alone. But if you get sick again, you're gonna go to bed and stay there. No arguing. Got that?"

"Go shoot something for supper!" She threw a rolled up blanket at him.

Clay stormed off through the brush talking to himself. "She needn't talk that way, when we're only trying to help. I wonder how she'd feel if we all just left her alone and made her do everything herself."

He shot and dressed a small mule deer near the opposite wall of the canyon, then took his sweet time lugging it back to camp. He dropped it at Teresa's feet with a firm nod.

"I killed something for supper. I hope it's good enough."

Chapter 14

The small deer was indeed good enough. Teresa sliced several nice-sized steaks and fried them with dried chilies and wild onions. Clay paused with a forkful of rice and beans halfway to his mouth as Antonio trotted into camp with the bloody carcass of a jackrabbit in his mouth. The dog dropped the creature beside Clay, then tore a chunk of meat and fur from the animal and chewed it.

"Yah! Get that outta here," he yelled, and kicked the rabbit into the dark. The dog cocked his head and gave Clay a puzzled look before trotting after his dinner.

"Don't be mad at him. He only wanted to join us for his supper," Teresa said as Julio and Estrella laughed.

"I ain't angry, but he can eat that critter somewhere else, where I don't have to see it."

"I watched him cut open the sage hen and pull its insides out last night and feed them to Antonio. Now, he complains because the dog killed his own dinner and chooses to eat with us," Julio said with a chuckle.

"At least I didn't gut that bird here in camp while we were trying to eat our dinner. There is a difference, you know."

Clay took a bite of rice and beans and chewed thoughtfully while he studied Teresa.

"By the way, how are you feeling?"

"Me?" Teresa asked.

"Yeah, you. You were sick this morning. I was just wondering how you're feeling?"

"I feel fine," she said with a shrug. She bit off a chunk of tortilla and turned toward Julio. "What do you plan on doing with your share of the gold?" she asked.

The vaquero shrugged and tilted his head to one side. "Buy a small place somewhere with cattle and horses. I haven't thought much about it. What do you plan, *señora*?"

"I would like to open my own restaurant and serve good food, so people don't have to eat the slop inside the cantina. That is what I've always wanted, but I don't think my husband likes the idea."

"I never said I didn't like the idee, it's just that I still want to buy a good ranch somewhere. I don't see why we can't have both, depending on how close our ranch is to town. It might work out fine. What about you, girl?"

"I have no plans," Estrella said with a shrug. I think I want a good life, with my own home and children. That is all."

Teresa smiled toward Julio and nodded, while the vaquero stirred the rice on his plate aimlessly.

Clay set his plate aside and took a sip of wine from a tin cup. "You know Leo's right about one thing. We are going to have to deal with that bunch camped downstream. It's just a matter of when."

"What do you think we should do?" Teresa asked.

"That's what I was hoping to hear from all ya'all. I think we should kick it around some and see what we come up with."

"We could slip down there tonight when they are sleeping and kill them all," Julio said with a crooked grin.

"That'd be plain murder, and I don't think any of us would like doing it any more than you believed I'd think it was a good plan."

Julio laughed and shoved a spoonful of rice into his mouth.

"Maybe they won't try to take the gold," Estrella said timidly.

"We can hope, but that ain't likely. It's gone this far, so you can bet your aunt Bessie's false teeth they'll come after the gold, once they're sure we've got it," Clay said. "When that happens, we'll have to fight to stay alive, 'cause they'll kill us all, if they can."

"Then, we will have to fight anyway. Why not do what Julio suggests," Teresa said.

"Because, if we kill them before they come after us, we'll be as guilty as they are. But once they try to rob us, it's a different poker game all together. What we need to do is make sure we're dealing the cards. We'll pick the time and place before it happens." Clay paused and pointed his fork toward Julio.

"What I'd like you and Estrella to do is, pick a trail that will afford us plenty of cover while we're toting the gold. We'll be moving slow, so we'll need every advantage we can get once the ball is opened. There's an old Indian trail I ran across yesterday, leading out of this canyon over yonder, behind the cottonwoods." Clay swung the fork to point. "It's steep and covered with slippery gravel, but I'm sure you can lead the horses and reach the top if you take your time. Teresa and me will let you two get a head start early tomorrow, then follow a day later. That should make those yahoos think we're still here, and you can slip away unseen. Think you can do that?"

"*Sí*," Julio said with a nod.

"Take a couple of water bags and some grub. If Teresa calculated right, you can cut our trail due west from here a day later."

******

Clay had just dozed off, but woke when he felt Teresa's warm lips against his ear as her right arm and leg snaked across his body.

"They are asleep. I can hear Julio's snores," she whispered.

He shifted to see her silhouette against the glow of the dying campfire.

"Estrella might still be awake."

"No, I think she is sleeping. And," Clay felt her hand as it explored the lower portion of his body, "she would not care."

"Dang, I thought you were mad at me for some reason."

"No, no," she said, kissing him on the lips. "Whatever gave you that idea?"

"The way you've been acting. I didn't think you'd be interested in making love."

"Ho, *señor*, you do not know your own wife."

He quit trying to reason things out, and figured her mood changes were simply the whims of a high-spirited woman. He pulled her body against his, accepting her advances.

Chapter 14

Leo sat perched on a rock eating the last of the three tortillas stuffed with rice and beans. He popped the last bite into his mouth and chewed vigorously, washing it down with a swig of brandy from a flask, then burped loudly.

"You are a pig," Manuel growled. "A real pig! You ate all three tortillas without giving a bite to anyone, even though you know we are hungry."

"Manuel, my friend," Leo said with a laugh, "there are twelve, and I only had three tortillas. How far would they have gone? I am not like *Jesus Cristo* who can feed a whole crowd with a few fishes and a little *pan*."

"No, but you could have given each of us one little bite."

"Then, no one would have been happy, my friend," Leo said. "This way, you might be angry, but I am happy."

"I am not your friend, Leo." Manuel pointed at him as he leaped to his feet. He patted the pistol on his hip. "I am not so sure who's side you are on. You ride into their camp and talk like old friends, then return with food. I should kill you now before you cause more trouble."

"Manuel, Manuel ..." Leo shook his head and clucked his tongue. "We have been through this before. You," he pointed toward Manuel, "are not fast enough, my friend. I would only kill you. You want to kill me? You would have to shoot me in the back or kill me in my sleep. That is why I am leaving your company." Leo walked slowly toward his horse and adjusted the cinches.

"If it is food you want, follow the creek upstream. You will find their camp, and Teresa will feed you. She sends no one away hungry, even if she plans to kill you later. You will at least die with a full stomach.

"But first," he motioned toward four riders approaching from the desert, "you might want to find out who your visitors are."

Leo swung into the saddle as Manuel spun on his heel to see the men approaching at an easy trot.

"*Adios*." Leo touched the brim of his sombrero before crossing the stream and urging his horse up the bank. He turned left, using several large boulders as protection, then galloped into the desert. He slowed the horse to a walk once he was sure he was out of gunshot range, and followed the canyon for a mile before stopping.

Leo swung to the ground and studied the tiny trail that led steeply down the canyon wall. There were fresh boot and dog prints in the sand. He turned and studied the desert, where the faint trail wandered through the scant brush and cactus, only to be swallowed by the wind-blown sand.

"Our friend Clay is quite the fox, isn't he, Amigo?" Leo said, rubbing the soft muzzle on his horse. "I was wondering how he planned on leaving the canyon without killing Manuel; now I know. This trail was probably used by Yaqui, but it now has become Clay Best's trail."

He led the horse to a flat, sandy area between several boulders and pulled the saddle and blankets.

"We'll camp here tonight and relax. I think we might see *Señor* Clay leave tonight, and we'll follow."

Leo snuggled against one of the boulders, wrapped in a saddle blanket. He woke early to the sound of crunching gravel and the whinny of a horse. He peeked around the boulder and grinned as Julio and Estrella appeared.

Sí, he thought. *Señor Clay is a foxy one.* He waited until Julio and the girl were out of sight, then followed.

Chapter 15

Manuel Rosales studied the four men as they trotted their horses upstream and stopped. He'd never seen them before. Two were white *Americanos,* one was a black man and the fourth a Mexican. The one in the lead pushed his dust-covered hat back as he surveyed the camp. Manuel unleashed his .45, then rested his hand against the butt as the man grinned.

"No need to take an unfriendly attitude, friend. We're just passing through." The man spoke softly as he removed his hat and wiped the sweatband.

"Then pass," Manuel barked and motioned toward the desert. "No one invited you, and and no one is stopping you."

"Now, I take that as being real un-neighborly." He turned in the saddle to look at the man on his right. "What do you think, Joe?"

"Yeah, I'd say he's a might on the testy side. I'd be willing to slap a little of that piss out of him, 'cept he's got a small army backin' him."

"What are you waiting for? I said you are not wanted," Manuel said as he drew his gun.

"Whoa, there partner." The man said holding his right hand in surrender. "We're leaving. As I said, we're just passing through. The reason we came here is because that creek just sort of dries up and disappears in the sand a little ways out." He motioned the way they had ridden. "Now, you've got some pretty good water here, and we're running a little shy. Just let us water the horses and fill our canteens and we'll be on our way."

Manuel glanced toward Miguel who nodded.

"*Bien*." Manuel said with a nod. "Then be gone."

"You don't have to tell me twice." The leader slid out of the saddle and filled his canteen. "Water's running kind of scarce out here. I ain't seen a rain cloud in weeks. I think coming to these parts was a big mistake." He finished filling the canteen and took a swallow before jamming the cork in with the palm of his hand.

"By the way," he paused to study Manuel with his foot in one stirrup, "the name is Red Simpson." He swung into the saddle. "I just thought you'd like to know, in case we ever run into each other again."

"What 'er all y'all out here for anyway?" Joe asked. "I know you're not out here for your comfort."

"I'm after the man who stole my woman," Wade Bailey said loudly. "He's camped right up the creek."

"Yeah?" Red said with a chuckle. "Hangin' around here ain't gonna get her back. Why don't you go get her?"

"Because he's a gunman, and he's got two more riding with him."

"Well hell, man," Joe said as his partners laughed. "You've got a dozen ridin' with you. Go get her and take her home."

"They don't care about her. They're just after the gold." Wade froze as Manuel jammed his pistol against his temple and cocked the hammer."

"Whoa," Red said. "Don't kill him yet. It was just getting interesting."

"You have your water, now go before I kill you all," Manuel said as the men in the campsite drew their guns. "And take this fat *gringo* with you." He gave Wade a shove.

"Okay, okay," Red said. He turned his horse and chuckled as Wade struggled to saddle his mare. "You'd best tell him to hurry up if he wants to ride with us." He nudged his horse's flanks and trotted back the way he'd come.

"Just keep moving, I'll catch up," Wade yelled as he tugged the cinches tight.

Chapter 16

Julio and Estrella set their horses into a ground-covering lope for several miles before settling to a gentle trot. They headed southwest in the direction that Teresa had said her old family homestead had been. The ground was mostly flat, not offering much cover for gold-laden mules. They would be easily overrun if he couldn't find a better way. They crossed a well worn military trail before turning westward toward the distant hills. Julio figured they must be directly north of Teresa's homestead when he spied an arroyo. Farther to the north, the ground appeared more uneven. He turned to investigate, hoping it would provide the exit-cover that Clay was seeking. They were approaching the arroyo, when a band of six Yaquis came out of the wash, encircling them in a wide ring.

"Keep your hands where they can see them, and don't make any threating moves," Julio said. He caught his breath as Estrella nudged her pony toward one particularly rough-looking brave. She spoke loud enough for all the braves to hear, in a mixture of Spanish and what he figured must be Yaqui. She gestured to Julio and the brave leaned slightly to peer around Estrella at him.

Hail Mary, full of grace; the Lord is with thee; blessed art thou among women and blessed is the fruit of thy womb, Jesus. Holy Mary, Mother of God, pray for us sinners, now and at the hour of our death. Amen. Julio made the sign of the cross as he mumbled the prayer, expecting a Yaqui arrow to slam into his back any second. Instead, the brave trotted his pony around Julio in a circle. Then he said something in Yaqui and nodded toward Estrella, who followed him into the arroyo. The remaining braves urged Julio into the arroyo behind them.

They traveled swiftly in the center of the wash for approximately two miles before exiting the arroyo and heading toward a pile of tumbled rocks and cactus. They compassed the hill for a quarter of a mile before the brave disappeared through a split in the rocks. Julio repeated the prayer as he followed Estrella through the split. They exited the narrow passageway into a large, sandy area where a small village of Yaqui were camped. Several children scampered to hide behind their mothers at the sight of the strangers. Estrella slid off her horse as a woman with gray hair came from a shelter made of brush and sticks. Estrella rushed to meet her, and was engulfed in the woman's arms. Julio jerked as one of the braves tapped him on the leg and motioned toward the ground. Julio dismounted and followed him toward several rocks, where the brave sat and patted the rock next to him.

Julio shrugged and sat, as Estrella followed the old woman into the shelter. Several children brought bowls of water and dried meat, then giggled and ran back toward brush huts. The water tasted of alkali and the meat was tough and salty, but Julio smiled and thanked the brave in Spanish as he chewed.

"She is her sister's daughter," the brave said in halting Spanish. "She has been gone a long time."

"Estrella lived here?" Julio asked.

"No. Her mother was Yaqui. Her father was Mexican. They lived in the village. He was crazy with the whiskey and sold Estrella after her mother died. Now she is home." The brave spoke mater-of-factly, glancing at the old woman's shelter.

"That is good," Julio said with a nod.

The brave left to speak with several others seated on animal skins and eating dried meat. Two of the children, a boy and a girl, returned to take the brave's place on the rock.

After Julio had finished the dried meat, and taken another sip of the salty water, the girl took his hand and led him around the village. She talked quickly, in a mixture of Spanish and Yaqui, making it difficult to understand. Julio smiled and nodded frequently. She was feeling important, especially when she introduced him to her friends. After showing him a small pool of water under the shelter of rocks, they returned to sit on the boulders and wait. After what seemed an eternity, Estrella and the old woman appeared. They embraced again as one of the braves brought their horses. She kissed the old woman and ran to grab Julio's hand.

"We go now," she said, pulling him off the rock.

They followed the braves back through the split in the rocks and toward the arroyo.

"The river and Texas," one of the braves said, pointing toward the north. "Apache and water that moans," he said pointing toward the south.

He trotted his pony around to face them.

"You go now," he said. He kicked the pony in the ribs and galloped away with the rest of the braves in a cloud of dust.

"*¿Qué fue eso?*" Julio asked, holding his horse in check as it side-stepped.

"My aunt is the village shaman. I tell them that you saved me from being sold, and that I am your woman and you treat me good. I also tell them the old gringo on the black horse with the woman on the red horse are my friends. I say that there are banditos looking to rob and kill us. The chief says they will not fight for us, but they will not harm you or *Señor* Best for my sake."

Estrella nudged her pony into the arroyo and turned toward the north. Julio guided his horse next to hers and studied her profile.

"What is the water that moans?" he asked.

"That is where *Señora* Best says the gold is hidden."

"You told them about the gold?" Julio asked.

"No, but I said *Señora* Best's family is buried there, and she wishes to say prayers over them. The chief says they do not go there much, because of the Apache. They are also afraid of the evil spirits that moan. He says there is water this way, but to be careful."

"We should meet *Señor* Best before we reach the water," Julio said.

"The chief says there is a village of Mexicans near the water. He says the people are not good and to be careful."

They rode in silence for the next hour, weaving around boulders and clumps of cactus. Julio raised his arm as his horse perked his ears and bobbed his head.

"*Alto Señorita*, he said.

They sat listening to the silence for about a minute before a deep wail drifted their way. Estrella looked up at Julio and smiled.

"Water that moans," she said.

They walked their horses for another half hour before dismounting to lead them past a small landslide of rocks and gravel. They exited the slide area and stood transfixed, staring at the green valley with a creek and waterfall. The ribbon of water ran from the fall and across the valley, where it seemed to disappear beneath the wall of rocks and gravel, not too far from where Julio and Estrella stood.

"*Señorita* Best's valley," Julio said.

"*Sí.*" Estrella nodded.

"Come, the horses are thirsty. We shall water them, then go to meet *Señorita* and *Señor* Best," Julio said, pulling his horse forward.

Chapter 17

Clay woke before daylight and gently nudged Teresa. She yawned and stretched before allowing her arm to drape around his neck. She gave him a quick kiss and grinned.

"*Buenos días, mi amor*, is it time?"

"Yeah, I changed our plans. I figure we oughta be out of here by the time those yahoos wake. It might put a kink in our meeting up with Julio and Estrella, but I don't want you and me to get pinned inside a boxed canyon if they decide they've waited long enough and come shootin'."

"*Bien.*" She kissed him once more and pulled her boots on.

Clay crawled out of the tent as Antonio stretched and shook his body violently, then trotted to a small bush and hiked his leg.

Teresa had the tent rolled and most of the gear packed by the time he returned with the horses and mules. They loaded the packs in silence without building a fire and making coffee. He saddled Loco and Diablo, then pulled three pieces of jerked beef from an oilskin. He handed one to Teresa and tossed one to Antonio as he swung into the saddle. They crossed the creek and wove their way slowly through the brush and small trees, following the canyon wall until the trail appeared. Clay dismounted and grinned.

"We'd best climb out on foot. It's steep and rocky," he said, as he handed the horses' reins to Teresa and took the lead rope to the mules.

"Let the horses have their lead. They'll figure what the best footing is."

"*Bien,*" she said with a nod and started up. The eastern sky had taken on a pink hue by the time they were halfway up the bank. Clay's legs were beginning to burn as Teresa and the horses disappeared over the rim.

"I don't know why I just didn't kill them sidewinders, and ride out of this hole, instead of sneaking off in the dark."

A cool breeze caught him as he crested the rim, and he had to jump aside as the mules bolted forward onto level ground. Clay wiped his brow and took a deep breath. The sun appeared to be a red crescent on the horizon. He turned to see Teresa bent over, holding her stomach.

"Are you okay?" He dropped the reins and reached for her.

"*Sí,*" she said with a forced smile. "It is just a little queasiness. I will be okay."

"I hope so. We'd better get mounted and head out of here. They might be able to see us from where they are."

They rode south past the canyon and into the flat desert for several miles, then turned southeast. They had ridden for approximately an hour before Clay called a halt. He dismounted and squatted, studying the ground, then walked several yards into the desert.

"What is it?" Teresa asked.

"It appears that Julio and Estrella have picked up some company. Take a look here," he said, pointing toward the tracks in the sand.

"See, here's Julio's horse, and here's Estrella's. This third set is fresher, maybe an hour or so later."

"Who is it?" She stared at him with wide eyes.

"I don't know. It's shod, so he ain't likely an Indian. We'd best keep a sharp eye until we figure who we're dealing with. I don't think whoever it is is up to any good."

They followed the tracks as the sun climbed higher. Clay called a halt mid-morning to rest the animals.

"It's gonna be a real scorcher today," he said, passing the canteen to Teresa.

"*Sí*," she said with a nod. "How are we going to find Julio and Estrella, now that we left early?"

"I figure they'll come looking for us at your valley, if we don't cross paths."

The sun rose higher and Clay's shirt clung to his body while sweat stung his eyes. He called another halt about midday and tied the mules and horses to a mesquite bush.

"Better rest awhile and get out of the sun," he said. Crawling under a second mesquite, Clay patted the ground next to him. Teresa removed her sombrero and crawled in next to him. Her hair hung plastered to her head.

"How are you making out?" Clay asked, passing her the canteen.

"*Bien*," she said with a nod. "I think there is a trail up there," she said pointing. "It goes to the small village I told you about.

"Well, I'd rather skip it altogether. We've already got too much company for my liking."

They lay back and closed their eyes, letting the warm breeze drift over them until Clay figured the animals had rested enough. He gave them a little water from one of the water bags, then helped Teresa into the saddle.

"How much farther to your canyon?"

"Mmm, another hour or two," she said with a shrug.

"Keep your eyes peeled and let me know if you see anyone," Clay said.

They rode in silence for half and hour before Antonio let out a loud bark. Clay pulled Loco to a halt, shading his eyes against the sun.

"Antonio sees two riders," Teresa said, pointing toward the south.

"Yeah, but I think we know them." Clay turned Loco toward the riders and nudged him into a trot. "I would have taken odds against meeting them this easily."

"Julio and Estrella?" Teresa asked.

"Looks like it." Antonio bolted past them barking happily and leaping over small brush and cactus.

"What do you think?" Clay asked.

"*Sí*, I think Antonio is happy to see them."

75

Chapter 18

They made a dry camp a half a mile off the trail in a small depression, thinking it might be safer to enter the canyon in the cover of early-morning darkness. Clay lit a lantern and was gathering sticks and hunks of wood to build a fire, when Antonio let out a low growl and barked several times. Clay took one look at the hair standing standing upright on the dog's neck and dropped the sticks. Loco and Diablo both snorted and danced uneasly.

"We've got some company, he said as Teresa poked her head out of the tent. She pulled one of her pistols, as Julio dropped the tent pole he was holding and grabbed his gun.

"You in the camp! Drop your guns and up with your hands. I've got a rifle aimed at your chest, big man. We've got four other guns on you, so just drop them, okay?"

Clay tossed the gun into the dirt and raised his hands. Teresa likewise tossed her pistol and took a step closer to Clay. Julio cursed and dropped his gun.

"Who are you, and what do you want? Show yourselves."

"Sure enough, partner, as soon as the little lady tosses that other iron. I ain't used to making myself a target."

Teresa pulled the other pistol and tossed it.

"That's much better. Where's the Injun gal? I don't see her."

Clay and Julio both glanced around the camp without seeing Estrella.

"Beats me," Clay said. I figured she was with this *vaquero.* I don't know where she is."

"Better come up with her real quick-like. My trigger finger is getting tired."

Clay and Julio both called her name several times to no avail.

"Like I said, I've go no idea where she went. She might've seen you coming and lit out. Now, why don't you show yourselves?"

"Sure. Just stand still. No sense in getting yourselves killed when there's no need."

Five men appeared as they stepped into the lantern light. Four were total strangers, but the fifth was the same man who claimed to have bought Estrella from her father.

"Okay, *hombres*, what is it you want from us?" Teresa said.

"Wall, for one thing," the leader said with a snicker, "I wouldn't mind having you. But what we really come for is those horses you folks have been riding. We ain't really looking to kill no one, but we had to leave Texas in a hurry, and our mounts are plumb wore out."

"Stealing a man's hoss is the same as killing him, in this country," Clay said.

"Maybe, but I could just kill you outright and keep the horses and the lady for myself, if that's what you want."

"You are out of luck, *señor*. You will never have me or my horse," Teresa hissed. "You will die here today."

The leader and two of the others roared in laughter.

"Now, that's what I like. A woman with spirit."

"Hey," yelled Wade Bailey. "Enough talking. Where's the girl?"

"Go find her, if you're that interested," growled the leader. "I'm tired of hearing about her."

"Well, I don't figure you're just gonna take our horses and leave us out here for dead. I figure you're gonna shoot us to make sure the job's done right," Clay said.

"Now, ain't that just like a Texan? You start out thinking the worst in a man before you even know him," the leader said. He then cocked his head to one side and chuckled. "But I think you've just about got it figured right."

"If I'm gonna die, how about letting me know who it is that's gonna do the killing?" Clay said.

"I guess there's no harm in swapping howdies before I bore you," the man said. He removed his hat to reveal a full-head of red hair.

"I'm Red Simpson. On the end is Joe Hopper. Say hello, Joe."

Joe nodded.

"Next is Amos Jones."

Jones grinned, revealing a set of broken and badly stained teeth.

"And then there's Pedro."

The Mexican was slender, about 5' 8", with sharp features, and a scar running along his left jaw. Clay decided the Mexican would be the most dangerous."

"Since you planned on killing us all along, why all the folderole? Why didn't you just plug us right off?"

"Well, I find it easier to get everyone in one spot first, and take their guns. Less chance of me or one of my men getting hurt. A man like you should appreciate that."

"Alright, where in the hell is she," Wade yelled, coming from inside the tent.

"Like I said, you want her? You find her," Red growled. He heaved a deep sigh and studied Clay.

"Na, I didn't figure you for a man that would surrender easily, and you ain't, are you?

"Not hardly," Clay said.

"Well, I reckon it's time to get 'er done," Red said, thumbing back the hammer on his pistol.

Clay grabbed for the revolver tucked inside his belt in back as Red swung his gun upward. Clay jerked the .44 free from his belt, but caught his breath as a shotgun roared from the darkness. Red was pitched backward with a large hole in his chest. Clay swung his gun toward the Mexican, but the Mexican was fast. As soon as Red went down, Pedro triggered a shot at Clay, barely missing him. Clay fired, hitting Pedro in the right hip. Pedro went down, but was able to get off another shot, taking Clay's hat, and burning his scalp. Clay fired twice more, hitting him in the chest and side.

Teresa hit the ground rolling, and came up with one of the .38s. She fired twice, hitting Amos in the right shoulder and in the chest. Julio had finished Joe Hopper, and turned his attention toward Wade Bailey, who had chosen to fire wildly as he ran. Julio fired two shots, missing with the first. The second shot hit Wade in the right shoulder. He took careful aim as Wade staggered, but another blast from the shotgun sent Wade sprawling in the dirt.

Estrella walked calmly into the light as she broke open the shotgun and inserted two new shells. Clay retrieved his hat and swatted at the dust before running his fingers across his scalp.

"I think I lost a little hair," he said to Teresa. "Dang it! I didn't have all that much to spare."

"*No es importante,*" Teresa said, as she wet a bandana with a canteen and dabbed at the wound. "I did not fall in love with your hair. Besides, we were lucky."

"Yeah, I figure we were. Reckon I'm the only one who got nicked." He studied Estrella as she joined them.

"You saved our bacon, little girl. Where'd you learn to shoot like that?"

Estrella stared at Teresa, who translated Clay's question into Spanish.

"She says she learned to shoot when she was a little girl. Her parents owned a small farm. Her father taught her to shoot birds and rabbits with a shotgun."

Estrella said something in Spanish that made Teresa laugh.

"What'd she say?" Clay asked, as he dabbed at the scalp wound and studied the bandana.

"She said her father's gun was not as big or powerful as this one. She says she likes your gun better."

"Well, tell her it's her gun now," Clay said.

Clay jammed his hat back on his head and wet the bandana once more before wringing it out and tying it around his neck.

"I hate to say this, but I figure none of us is gonna get much sleep tonight. Besides, we're not that far from that village up yonder, and someone might have heard our ruckus. There's a good chance some folks will come to investigate. We'd better see what these yahoos have on them and mosey down the road."

"*Esta bien*," Julio said with a nod and knelt beside Red Simpson. Clay and Julio quickly searched all five men's pockets, while Teresa and Estrella packed and loaded the mules. Red Simpson had a small photograph that look slightly like Roberta Sawyer, and Clay found a pendant and wedding band on Pedro. All together, there was close to five hundred dollars in American currency, and one hundred and seventy pesos. Wade Bailey had very little, other than a few papers and a twenty-dollar gold piece. Clay figured he wasn't part of Red's gang, but only after Estrella.

"Well, you finally got her," he said, staring down at the crumpled body. "I don't think you got what you expected, but you got her." He looked at what Julio had found and shrugged. "I don't see any letters or address books, so I don't guess anyone's going to be writing a letter to a wife or ma, saying Junior's not coming home."

Clay and Julio pulled the saddles from the bandits' horses and set them free.

"Let's mount up and mosey down the road," Clay said and he swung into the saddle. He turned toward Teresa and heaved a sigh. "Well, which way is your valley?"

"We go there now?"

"Might as well. It can't be more trouble than we've already had. I'm thinking we should've stayed back in Carrizo Springs, and forgotten about the gold."

He nudged Loco in the sides and turned south. Teresa trotted Diablo next to him and pushed her sombrero to the back of her head.

"My *marido muy fuerte* isn't quitting, is he?"

"I didn't say that," Clay snapped. "And while you might think of me as your *very strong husband*, I almost got you killed tonight, by letting those highbinders sneak up on us. I already lost one wife, and I don't want to lose you too. That's all I am saying."

They rode in silence for several minutes before Teresa shook her head and chuckled.

"Look at me," she said, swatting his arm. "That was not your fault. Those men sneaked up on all of us...me, you, Julio and Estrella. Antonio did not bark until it was too late. The wind came from the other way, and he didn't smell them. It was not your fault."

"Maybe, but one more incident like tonight, and we're packing it in and heading home. Gold or no gold. Got that?"

"*Sí*," she said with a nod. "But others will come after we have the gold. What will you do then? Throw the gold on the ground and run?

Clay halted his horse and glared at her. Julio and Estrella stopped their mounts and watched from a safe distance.

"Now, that's a damned stupid statement, if I've ever heard of one. They come at us after we've gone through this much trouble, you can be damned sure I'll fight."

"*Bien*," she said with a nod. "But if we are going to my valley, we have to go this way. The way you are going will be a long ride to Mexico City" She turned Diablo east and trotted into the night.

"Damned woman, anyway," Clay growled and spurred Loco after her.

Chapter 19

Teresa pulled up Diablo and dismounted near a small burnt-out homestead. The house made of adobe and stone still had three walls standing. Clay could hear the roar of rushing water as he dismounted.

"Come," she said, leading the horse inside. "We are very close to a trail used by animals that leads to the falls. It is the trail we will use, but it is dangerous in the dark. We will wait until there is enough light, then we will go."

"The trail Estrella and I used is not too far that way," Julio said, pointing toward the north.

"*Sí*, but it is sandy, and we will leave tracks. The small trail is rocky, and the antelope and burros will come and hide our trail."

"Sounds good to me," Clay said. "We've got about two hours 'til sunup. Might as well leave the animals saddled and packed. Any chance we can make some coffee?"

Teresa and Estrella made a sparse breakfast of coffee, jerked beef and stale tortillas. Clay spent the rest of the night perched in one of the windows with his rifle cradled in his lap. He nudged the others awake when the eastern sky first showed pink. Teresa led the way through rock and brush, staying within a hundred yards of the canyon rim. She stopped Diablo after a quarter mile and leaned in the saddle, studying the ground, then moved on, stopping a little further to repeat the action. Then she motioned the others to follow as she turned toward the canyon.

Clay stopped Loco and sat transfixed, staring at the rushing stream below. A cool mist carried on the morning breeze floated upward to caress their faces. Teresa dismounted and held Diablo in check as he danced nervously.

"It is dangerous from here on," she said. "It is slippery and better to walk and lead the horses. We must hurry, because the animals inside will come out soon to hide from the Indians and farmers who hunt this valley."

Clay dismounted and took the lead rope for one of the mules, then handed the other to Julio.

"Everyone had best hold on tight; the animals are thirsty and smell water," he said.

Teresa led the way down slowly, sticking toward the middle of the small trail. Clay could reach out and touch the water cascading over the rim as it gushed downward to the valley. He tried asking her where exactly the cave was located, but the sound of the water drowned his words before they reached her ears.

Teresa suddenly turned into the fall and dissappeared. Clay stopped when he reached that point to see a ledge, just wide enough for a horse, curving behind the cascading water. Diablo's rear quarters could be seen a few yards ahead, before dissappearing into an opening in the rock wall. He yelled and grumbled, trying to get Loco to follow the red horse. He finally allowed the mule to go first, then, for some unknown reason, the horse decided to follow.

The opening in the rock was narrow, but opened into a wide cavern. Clay pulled the mule and horse farther inside, giving room as Estrella and her pony appeared. They were followed shortly by Julio and the rest of the animals. The cavern was cool and damp, and black as pitch a few yards away from the waterfall. The mules fought the lead rope and voiced their protest against the blackness. A small light flared as Teresa struck a match and lit a lantern. The light grew brighter as she lit a second.

"Here, you and Estrella unpack the animals, while I go clear our tracks," Clay said, handing the vaquero the reins.

He broke a green leafy branch from the backside of a greasewood bush near the fall and climbed back up the trail. He worked his way back down, sweeping their prints and horse droppings from the trail. The animals were unpacked by the time he returned, and the women were busy making ready their campsite.

Clay and Julio brought in grass and leafy branches for the horses and mules, then gave them nosebags of oats. A steady trickle falling from the roof of the cavern had created a pool of cold water the animals found inviting. They gathered dry sticks and branches from a dead mesquite, being careful to sweep their tracks, and Teresa built a small fire to cook breakfast. Clay sat on his bedroll sipping coffee and watching the smoke from the fire as it drifted deeper into the cave and disappeared.

"There must be another enterance to this cave," he said thoughtfully.

"*Sí*," Teresa said. "That is what Refugio believed." I have never seen it, but the cave does not moan until the wind comes from the west. Then it makes the noise that frightens the Indians."

"It might be good for me and Julio to see if we can find it. It could be another way out after we find the gold."

They finished a late breakfast of coffee, tortillas and dried beef. Julio said he would shoot an antelope later, if they thought it safe. Antonio came trotting in with a rabbit and found a comfortable spot to devour his meal.

"Too bad we didn't teach him to hunt for us," Clay said with a shrug. "That would solve the fresh meat problem."

"Maybe you should teach him when we get home," Teresa said with a giggle.

"Maybe." He tossed the remnants of his cup and stretched with a yawn. "You got any idee where Refugio might've hid the gold?"

"*Sí*," she said, pointing toward a large pile of rocks and boulders at the far end of the cavern. "He said it is buried on the opposite side under rocks and gravel."

"Hum, that's a pretty big pile. We might have to do some digging. But first, I think I'm going to get some shut-eye. Julio," he said to the vaquero, "you get the first watch. We'll haul in more feed for the animals this afternoon and decide on who gets to stay up most of the night."

****

He woke several hours later to find Julio and Antonio perched on a boulder, behind a clump of mesquite and greasewood, watching the canyon.

"See anyone coming or going?" he asked.

"No," Julio said, shaking his head. "Antonio growls once, but I think it was at a coyote that comes down the trail. He hears Antonio and runs back up the hill."

"That's good. Maybe our leaving early threw them off."

"Maybe."

Clay retreated back inside and took one of the lanterns to the pile of rocks to look for any sign of digging.

Finding none, he slipped on his gloves and began rolling the larger rocks to one side. He had just finished moving a rather large one when Teresa appeared and threw her weight against a small boulder with a grunt.

"Here," Clay said, easing her aside. "You shouldn't bc doing that."

"And why not?" she said, pushing him aside. "I am not helpless, *señor*."

"You've been feelling poorly. Besides, there's no need of you getting all bruised and banged up. Julio and I can move the big ones."

"So can we," she said with a grin as Estrella joined her. Both women rolled the rock aside with grunts, then stood back with a look of great pride.

"Okay, just don't bung your back up. We've gotta ride out of this place sooner or later."

They finally gave up after two hours of hard labor and sat on their bedrolls sipping water from the canteens.

"Maybe you were looking in the wrong place," Julio said.

"Refugio said it is under a pile of rocks at the far end of the cavern," Teresa insisted.

"Maybe, but there is more than one pile of rocks," Clay said. "Let's rest and try again later. Right now, we're tired and not thinking straight."

"*Esta bien,*" Teresa said. "Now, it is time to fix supper."

Chapter 20

Manuel Rosales crept carefully upstream, moving from rock to rock, bush to bush. Each move took him closer to the gringo's campsite. They had not heard the big yellow dog bark, nor the sound of an ax or the shotgun, or smelled their campfire for an entire day. It was impossible for them to ride out of the valley unseen, because to do so, they would have to pass his own campsite. He became even more cautious and moved slower the closer he came. Finally, when he knew he was close enough, he waited for what seemed an eternity. There was no chatter of women's voices, no smell of a fire or cooking food. There was also no barking dog. *Impossible*, he thought.

Standing upright, Manuel could not believe his eyes. There in plain view was the the ring of rocks for the campfire, but there were no horses or people anywhere.

He cursed loudly as he ran toward the abandoned camp. Still seeing nothing, he cursed again, as he dashed across the creek to the clearing where the horses and mules had been kept. He could see the droppings and where the animals had cropped the grass and the bark and leaves from several shrubs, but they were gone. He spun at the sound of a boot against the gravel to point his gun at Miguel.

"Whoa, it is me, *hombre*," Miguel said. "Where have they gone?"

"Where have they gone? That is what I want to know." Manuel stomped around the clearing, waving his arms like a wild man. "Horses and mules can't fly. There has to be another way out that we don't know about."

"But Leo said downstream was the only way."

"Then Leo lied. And where is Leo? Do you see him?"

"No, you ran him off," said Miguel timidly.

"And rightfully so. He was a traitor," Manuel shouted. "I think he rides with them, and I will kill him next time I see him."

Miguel watched as Manuel stomped downstream cursing loudly.

Chapter 21

Leo Santiago sat on his heels studying the faint animal trail and grinned. He had been following from a distance, keeping downwind and making sure not to alert the dog. Teresa had taken the lead early that morning, and it had been difficult to follow. Up to now, he had been able to follow the tracks left by the mules and horses. But Teresa had stayed to the rocky ground, carefully picking her way through brush and cactus, and leaving very little for him to follow. It had been pure luck that the sun had risen high enough for him to see the riders disappear over the rim of the canyon, or he would have ridden past the trail.

Leo's eyes scanned the trail and the green valley below. It was not a large valley by any imagination, but it was lush with grass and small trees. And more importantly, it had water, which was a scarce commodity after three years of drought. If it were not for the Indians who frequented the area, it would have been a perfect place to build a home and raise a family.

His eyes traveled back and forth across the valley, finding no sign of Clay Best or the others. He pushed his sombrero to the back of his head and grinned. It seemed as though the band of two men and two women had disappeared, taking their horses and mules with them. But that was not possible.

"This Clay Best and his woman are sly ones, aren't they, Amigo," he said to the horse. "We are going to have to wait until they make themselves known."

He had hardly gotten the words out of his mouth when Clay appeared out of the waterfall. He had a leafy branch in his hand and was climbing up the trail toward him. Leo quickly backed away, leading his his horse toward a small boulder that was sheltered with a scrub pine and some mesquite.

"Shhh, Amigo," he whispered, placing a hand against the horse's muzzle. "Let's see what he is doing."

He peered through the mesquite as Clay appeared cautiously over the canyon rim to glance around. Seeing no one, he began swiping as he descended back down the trail. Leo tied his horse to the mesquite and ran silently to the head of the trail. He peered carefully through the brush as Clay backed down the trail.

Clay suddenly stopped when he reached the waterfall and took another look around. Leo's heart skipped a beat as the man seemed to stare right at him for an instant. Clay gave no indication that he either saw him or sensed his presence. Then he turned and disappeared into the waterfall.

"*Santa Maria, Madre de Dios,*" Leo said, standing upright. He stared at the waterfall, not believing what he had just seen. It was not a large fall with a great volume of water, but it was enough to knock a grown man off his feet. He rejoined his horse at the boulder.

"Yes this is proving to be fun, Amigo. I think Clay Best and his woman are far smarter than I gave them credit. I also think that the waterfall is where the gold is hidden. It's going to be our job to watch, and make sure they're not disturbed. Well, we shall make sure they arrive in Texas safely with the gold. Then we shall ask for what is ours."

Chapter 22

Julio shot a small antelope that afternoon and dressed the carcass behind a mound of boulders at the base of the fall. Clay helped him haul the meat into the cave and store it wrapped in an oil skin inside a small branch of the cavern. Then the men took turns keeping watch while the other cut a dead tree into manageable hunks and carted it inside.

They left Antonio with a hunk of the antelope at the mouth of the cave and washed for supper. Teresa and Estrella cooked the meat as Clay sat on a boulder, watching the smoke disappear.

"Here, I'm gonna try something," he said after a few minutes. He set his cup aside and grabbed his rope, handing one end to Julio.

"I'm gonna take one of the lanterns and follow that smoke. I want you to give a jerk on the rope when I get near the end, then I want you to tie your rope to mine and give another jerk. Keep doing that 'till I find where the smoke is going, or we run out of rope."

"*Bueno*," Julio said with a nod, and began feeding rope to Clay as he disappeared deeper inside the cave. He was on his third coil of rope when the tension became slack. They waited for what seemed an eternity before they heard the crunch of Clay's boots against the cavern floor and saw the glow of the lantern.

"Well, I found it," Clay said, coming into the light of the campfire. "It might take some work, but I was able to squeeze outside, and I figure we could get out that way in a pinch. Getting the horses and mules out might be another story."

"Are you saying we have to leave our horses? Teresa said.

"Now, all I'm saying is, it would take a lot of work to clear rock and make the hole larger before getting the animals through. On the other hand, if those highbinders found us, and had us penned inside this cave, we could get out the other end and make a fight of it."

"*Bien*," Teresa said with a nod. "That is good to know. Your supper is ready as soon as you wash your hands and face."

Julio snickered as Clay scowled.

"You too Julio," she added. "Both of you are dirty, and I will not have you eating with us until you are clean."

"Go," Estrella said, pointing toward the pool.

Chapter 23

Leo made a decision to ride to the village and find a place to spend the night. He was hungry and he knew his horse need decent feed before the long dry journey back to Texas. He left the horse at the stable and rented a space to sleep at a small casa at the end of town, figuring the widow living there needed the pesos more than the cantina.

He bathed and changed his cloths, then walked to the cantina. He was seated at a window table when he saw them enter town. The gang was much smaller now, no more than ten men, but it seemed that Manuel Rosales was still in charge. He could not hear what they were saying, but it didn't take much imagination to figure Manuel was not in a good mood. He was ranting and waving wildly. Even Miguel Villa rushed, taking Manuel's horse by the reins and hurrying toward the stable.

Leo drained the *cerveza* in his mug and ambled toward the rear door. It wasn't that he was afraid to face Manuel Rosales by any stretch, but the village happened to lay on a road frequented by the Federales, and killing a man who had just ridden into town might be frowned upon if they happened to be near.

Leo circled several buildings on his way toward the widow's casa, staying out of sight. He planned to rise early and return to his lookout near the waterfall. He didn't believe Clay and Teresa knew exactly where Refugio had hidden the gold, but he wanted to be near, in case he was wrong. He removed his sombrero as he stepped into the cool shade of the adobe casa.

"*Buenas tardes, señora*," Leo said with his best smile. "I wonder if I might impose on you to feed me while I stay here. I was at the cantina, and their food didn't look like it was healthy."

"*Sí*," the old woman said weakly. "I do not have much, but I am happy to share."

"I am sure what you have will be wonderful. Besides," Leo gently placed a gold coin in her palm, "I'd rather give this to you than those men who run the cantina."

"Oh, *señor*, that is too much," she said, trying to give it back to him.

"No, that is yours, *señora*. I insist." He smiled and squeezed her knarled hand. "Besides, you can buy food to feed us both. I need to rest, and I may stay here several days, if that is okay."

"*Bien*," she said with a nod.

"Oh, one more thing," Leo said as she started to leave. "Don't tell anyone about me. There are some men in town who tried to rob me a few days ago. If they knew I was staying here, they would come to steal my money, and they might even hurt you. *Bien*?"

"*Sí*," she said with a smile.

Leo rolled a cigarette as he watched her walking slowly down the street, using a cane. It was likely more money than the poor woman had seen in months, or maybe a year. He had a good feeling inside as he struck a match and touched it to his smoke. Wasn't there something about taking care of widows written in the Bible? Perhaps God would send a blessing his way for this small deed.

Chapter 24

Clay straightened his back with a moan and mopped the sweat from his brow with his bandana. They had been moving rock and gravel for six hours straight without success. Teresa had experienced another bout of heaving earlier, and now the frustration and strain of not finding where Refugio had hidden the gold was beginning to show on her brow.

"Let's take a break and cogitate the situation." He handed Teresa a canteen of water before submerging his own head in the pool of water. Clay then sat on a small boulder and combed his hair back with his fingers. He was beginning to think Estrella had sensed what they were up against when she volunteered to take the first watch.

"*Gracias*," Teresa said, handing him the canteen. "I don't understand," she said, shaking her head. "Refugio said the gold was buried under a pile of rocks on the opposite side of the cavern."

"Maybe it is," Clay said. He took a long swig from the canteen and passed it to Julio. "But it seems we are looking under the wrong pile. Anyone got any ideas?"

Teresa lowered her head while Julio sat in silence.

"Neither do I."

They sat several more minutes before he stood and stretched his back.

"Tell me once again what Refugio told you."

"I already tell you a dozen times," Teresa snapped, and waved her arm in frustration.

"I know he said it was under some rocks on the opposite side of the cavern, and that's more'n likely true. But the fact remains, there are several piles of rock. I suppose we could move them all, if we have a mind to. But I'd rather not."

Teresa set her lips into a straight line as she glared at him.

"Just this once," Clay said, gently laying his hands on her shoulders. "Think real hard and tell me exactly what Refugio said about the gold."

Teresa took a deep breath and exhaled loudly, then sat on the boulder and cradled her chin in her palms with her elbows against her knees.

"He said that he and three revolutionaries hided the gold inside this cave. He said it took a wagon to bring the gold, so they left one man at the top of the trail while the others carried it down the animal trail. Then, they all buried it here."

"I believe you," Clay said softly as he sat beside her. "What did he say when he told you where they hid it. Think hard, and tell me exactly."

"He said, they buried it under some rocks on the opposite wall."

"The wall opposite of what?"

Teresa's head snapped up and she stared at him with a smile.

"He said the wall opposite the water falling." She laughed and jumped to her feet. "I think he meant the waterfall but," she ran to the pool, "I think now he means this." She held out her hand to catch the small drizzle falling from the roof.

Clay joined her at the pool and held his lantern high, studying the dark cavern.

"I think you might be right," he said, and walked slowly toward the rock wall. A rock shelf running about five feet from the floor contained several large rocks that looked too perfect to have been created by nature.

"Julio, come give me a hand," he said as he grabbed one of the rocks and gave it a toss.

The vaquero hurried to move another one. Teresa stood transfixed as the men gave rock after rock a toss, then suddenly stopped. Clay grabbed the lantern, placed it on the shelf, and glanced at Julio. The vaquero seemed hypnotized as Clay reached into a small opening in the wall.

"Here," he called to Teresa. "It's fitting you get the first one. He placed a gold coin in her palm.

"It is there?" she asked, staring at the shiny coin.

"You bet it is," Clay said, dumping a handful of coins into her palms.

They pulled several more handfuls from the opening before Julio was able to drag a torn money bag to the floor. Teresa scooped the scattered coins into a small pile as they pulled several large sacks into the open. They finally stopped to catch their breaths.

"It is too much, *Señor* Clay," Julio said. "There is much more, and what we have is heavy. The mules won't be able to carry it all."

"I sort of figured that might be the case," Clay said hoarsely. "I'm thinking we'll take what we know they can handle, and bury the rest like Refugio. We can always come back and get the rest later."

"*Sí,*" he said with a nod.

"*Señor* Clay, *Señor* Clay," Estrella said as she rushed inside the cave. "Come quick and see."

Clay laid a hand against Antonio as the dog growled. He crept from behind the fall and slowly parted the branches of a greasewood as Julio joined him.

"Apaches," Clay said with a curse. There were a dozen Indians gathered at the stream about a hundred yards from the waterfall.

"*Sí,* Mescalero. They are going to make camp tonight. See?" Julio pointed toward two braves carrying a small elk into camp as another built a ring of stones for a campfire. "They will spend the night here before moving on."

"What do you think? Raiding party or huntin'?"

"Raiding," Julio said with a nod. "They have war paint."

"Reckon they are heading for Texas?" Clay turned toward the vaquero.

"*Sí*, Texas. They will raid the villages and farms before coming back to Mexico. They are taking the same trail we were going to take."

"Figures. We'll need to keep our eyes peeled once we leave the cave." Clay turned back inside the cavern mumbling.

"That's all we need. We've got a bunch of highbinders after the gold, Yaqui Indians running around God knows where, and now 'paches looking to take our hair. What's gonna be next? Federales? It wouldn't surprise me."

Chapter 25

Manuel Rosales leaned over the corral and stared at the chestnut.

"Pedro says this is Leo's horse," Miguel Villa said as he rolled a cigarette. "I asked the stable boy, and he said he didn't know the owner's name, but the description he gave sounds a lot like Leo."

"How long has he been here?" Manuel asked.

"The boy said the rider left the horse about three hours before we arrived. We just didn't notice. I think Leo is somewhere in the village."

"Then we shall find him," Manuel yelled. "Gather the men and search every *jacale* until you find him. I want to see him personally, before I kill him."

******

Leo Santiago had decided to leave his horse this morning and walk the two miles to his hideout at the rim of the canyon. After watching the waterfall for several hours with no sign of Clay or those with him, he decided to return to the widow's house and rest. He was nearing the *jacale* when he saw Miguel Villa standing outside the front door with three others. Leo loosed the leather lash on his pistol and approached cautiously. He could hear Manuel's booming voice before Miguel and the others noticed him. Leo held out his left hand, motioning Miguel to stand still.

"Manuel," Leo called out. "There is no need to bother *Señora* Rohas. I am here in the yard with Miguel."

"So, you finally decide to show yourself, when you've been hiding with this old woman like the coward you really are," Manuel bellowed as he drug the old woman outside.

"Hiding?" Leo laughed as he came closer. "Leo Santiago may do a lot of things, but hiding is not one of them. But I will promise this," he pointed a finger toward Manuel, "if you continue to hurt *Señora* Rohas, I will kill you." He circled the drunken bandit, inching closer, until he thought the widow was out of danger.

"Ha! That's big talk coming from a coward," Manuel bellowed. He caught his breath as Leo drew and cocked his pistol inches from his face.

"Does that look like something a coward would do, Manuel? I've never been afraid of you. I haven't killed you, because it will be fun to watch Clay Best do that for me. But, if you do not take your filthy hands off *Señora* Rohas, I will kill you now, in front of God and everyone." The widow gasped as Leo stepped closer and jammed the .45 against Manuel's head. "What will it be, Manuel?"

Manuel let the widow loose and stepped back.

"Ah-ah," Leo said as a young *vaquero* reached for his pistol. "Don't make me kill you, Chico. There's no need of dying because Manuel is stupid."

Leo lowered the pistol, as the widow disappeared inside, but held it against his leg, cocked.

"Clay and Teresa are not far from here," he said. "I think they have found the gold, and will be moving shortly. You can either die here now, or you can take your horses and try to find them."

"Yeah? Where are they, if you know so much?" Manuel growled.

"In a valley about two miles south. They may have already gone," Leo said with a grin. "I was there, and came back to get my horse. The boy at the stable told me you were here. So, what are you going to do?" Leo pointed the gun at

Manuel once more. "Shall I kill you, or do you want to find Clay and Teresa?"

"We shall go," Manuel said, pointing his finger at Leo. "But, after I have killed the old gringo and taken the gold, I will come back and kill you."

"You are welcome to try, Manuel, but I won't be here. I will be near Clay and Teresa, watching and waiting."

"Waiting for what?"

Leo laughed loudly and shook his head. "Waiting to watch Clay Best kill you. Now go, before I get tired of waiting and kill you myself."

He waited until he was sure they were heading toward the stable before stepping inside. He took the widow by the hands and smiled gently.

"I am sorry for that display, *Señora* Rohas. I never wanted you to see that or be in any danger."

"Were those the men you told me about?" she asked.

"*Sí*," Leo said with a nod. "They are bandits, and they think nothing of killing someone to take a few pesos. I am a peaceful man, *señora*, and I don't want to kill them, but I may have to, if they attack my friends who are in the valley."

"The old gringo that man said he was going to kill is your friend? Why did you tell him where he is?" She crinkled her brow and pulled away.

"Because, that gringo isn't just an old man. The gringo is Clay Best, and he was a marshal in Texas. He will kill Manuel Rosales and the members of his gang. Besides, *señora*," he added with a laugh, "I did not tell them where *Señor* Clay is. The valley I sent them to was empty when I looked. I think they may be gone. If they're not gone, they soon will be."

Chapter 26

Clay kept watch, hidden behind the greasewood, while Julio and Teresa hid the remaining gold. A gust of wind sent a tumbleweed dancing through the Apache camp. One of the braves caught the weed and used part of it for kindling to start the campfire. Clay poked his head inside the cave as the clacking of metal horseshoes against stone floated his way. Estrella was busy trying to calm the animals as they danced nervously.

"Hold 'em still," he ordered, as Julio's horse whinnied.

"I try, *Señor* Best," the girl cried.

"Here," Clay growled as he reached for the lead rope. Then a different sound caused him to freeze. He glanced toward Teresa and Julio at the far end of the cavern, to find them staring back. It wasn't like anything he had heard before. It started like a low moan, rising slowly, then fading, only to return seconds later.

"It is the cave," Teresa said. "Her spirit is moaning with the wind."

Clay rushed back to the greasewood and parted the branches. Several more tumbleweeds skipped across the ground as the branches on the mesquites danced with the wind.

"Where in the hell did the wind come from?" he grumbled as Teresa joined his side.

"It comes quickly sometimes and causes the cave to make noise. See," she said, pointing toward the canyon floor. "The Apache hear the cave moan."

A large gust of wind caused the cave to wail loudly like a beast in pain. The frightened mules stamped wildly and brayed loudly. The braying of the mules, mingled with the howling of the cave, created an unearthly sound that rose and fell with the gusting wind, causing the hair on Clay's neck to stand on end.

"The cave's not all they're likely to hear," Clay said as he dove into the cave and grabbed one of the mules. His efforts to quiet the frightened animal only caused him to bray louder and thrash about, which made the horses whistle and neigh.

"Dammit!" He was close to shooting the mule when Teresa started tugging on his arm.

"Not now," he hissed at her. "We've gotta quiet the animals or them 'paches will be taking our hair."

"No, no, no," she said, tugging harder. "They are leaving. Come and see."

"What?" He pulled back.

"The Indians are leaving," she said excitedly. "Come see."

She tugged on his arm again and Clay let go of the mule to follow. She pulled the branch back and pointed. Clay took one peek and turned to stare at Teresa, then turned back to the Indians below. The were leaving hurriedly, forgetting the roasting elk on the campfire.

"See, I told you they are leaving," Teresa said with a smile.

"Yeah, but why?"

"I think they hear the mules crying with the cave, and they think an evil spirit lives here. I don't think they will come again," she said. She turned and called for Julio and Estrella, but the cave and mules drowned her words.

"They can't hear you. You're gonna have to go get them," Clay said, then laughed as she disappeared inside. Julio came quickly and peered through the bush, shaking his head.

"It is true, *Señor* Clay. The Indians are leaving."

"Sure enough," Clay said as the last brave disappeared over the rim of the canyon. "You might want to rescue that elk roasting down there. I think that solves supper worries tonight."

Clay patted Julio on the back and laughed as the cave continued to moan.

"I don't know how in the hell we're gonna sleep with all that racket. But at least we won't go hungry."

******

Teresa and Estrella took care of the elk while Clay and Julio took one of the saddles and several blankets and followed the rope to the opening at the far end of the cave. The wailing noise turned into howling wind the closer they got.

"Here, hand me the saddle first," Clay said, positioning himself near the hole. He stuffed the saddle into the hole, then packed blankets tightly around it, then piled several rocks to keep them in place.

"Reckon that ought to do it," he said, dusting his hands against his pant legs.

They could hear Teresa and Estrella coughing as they neared the entryway. The cavern was quickly filling with smoke.

"The moaning stopped, but now we have smoke," she said.

"Huh, that's one I never figured on," Clay said.

"Do something." Teresa coughed again.

"Give a tug on the rope when you see the smoke clearing," he told Julio, then started back down the long passageway.

Clay set the lantern on a rock and pulled a blanket from the hole. He waited a minute or two then pulled another. He had just pulled the third blanket when he felt a tug on the rope. He tugged the rope and started back. He met the smoke halfway and covered his nose and mouth with a handkerchief. His eyes were tearing when he stepped into the cavern. It took him a minute to clear his eyes after washing his face in the pool. He wiped it with the bandana and turned. The nearness of Teresa's face caused him to jump.

"*Perdóname*," she giggled. "I did not mean to frighten you."

"I just didn't expect you to be standing that close, that's all," Clay said with a crooked grin. "Something wrong?"

"No," she shook her head, "I just wanted to say *gracias* for making the smoke go away." She gave him a quick kiss.

"You're quite welcome."

He watched her slim body as she moved about the campfire, making coffee. It had been a little over a week since they had been alone, and he didn't particularly like an audience while making love to his wife. He desperately missed holding her body against his, and feeling her soft skin with his fingers. It might be a cold day in hell before he'd ever return to fetch the rest of the gold. Feeling Teresa was more important.

Chapter 27

Manuel Rosales was fuming by the time the horses were saddled, then things grew worse. Pedro was drunk and barely able to stay in the saddle. Joaquin had vomited down the front of his clothes, so Miguel threw him into one of the watering troughs, which incurred the wrath of the stable owner.

"What are you trying to do, poison the horses? They have to drink that water."

Manuel grabbed his gun with every intention of killing the man, but Miguel held his arm.

"Hold on, *amigo*. We might want to stable our horses again before we're through. Besides, killing him would only make the villagers angry."

"Who cares about the damned peasants who live here?"

"We would, if all seventy-five men and women came upon us at one time. *Bien*?" Miguel grinned.

Manuel took a deep breath and exhaled slowly. "*Bien. Bien.*"

They traveled at a slow trot, and Manuel fell deeper into a sullen state. He had decided to kill half of them by the time they were close enough to hear the roar of the waterfall. A big yellow dog saw them coming and barked loudly before disappearing over the rim to bound down a narrow trail.

"*Amigo*," Miguel said, grabbing Manuel's arm. "Wasn't that Teresa Romero's dog that has been following them?"

"Hell, how do I know who that dog belongs to?" Manuel barked. "I'm not trying to find a dog. I'm trying to find a wagon-load of gold."

"*Sí,*" Miguel said with a nod. "But if we find the dog, we will find Teresa and the gold."

Manuel stared at his friend with a blank expression, then grinned and swatted his arm.

"*Sí,*" he laughed, "*sí,* you are right, of course." He galloped to the edge of the canyon and dismounted, then surveyed the canyon floor several times before turning to yell at Miguel.

"Where in the hell's that dog? He can't fly! We saw him run into the canyon right here. Where are they?"

Miguel dismounted and studied the green landscape with a silver ribbon of water below him.

"No, dogs don't fly, my friend. But they do hide. They are here, hiding somewhere below, or the dog would not still be here. *Bueno*? So, we wait. Once they have the gold, they will have to leave. Then we will be waiting."

Manuel laughed loudly, and punched Miguel in the arm. "*Bueno,* my friend, *bueno.*" He turned to yell at the motley members of his gang.

"Dismount! All of you. You are drunken fools who aren't worth shooting." He grabbed Joaquin by the shirt, dragging him from the saddle. The man fell to the ground with a heavy thud.

"I ought to shoot all of you. Miguel is the only one of you who is worthy of the gold."

"*Jefe,* what do you want us to do?" Pedro pleaded weakly.

"What do I want you to do? Why should I have to tell you what to do." He slapped the hung-over vaquero on the side of the head. "You should know what I want you to do."

He stomped to the center of the group and yelled. "I want you to unsaddle your horses and make a camp, right here." He pointed toward his feet.

"But *jefe*, wouldn't it be better to make the camp over there, in the rocks? We would be out of the sun and the wind," Pedro said. The vaquero backed away quickly when the leader jerked around to glare at him.

"You want shelter? You want to be out of the sun and the wind? How about I shoot you and throw your bodies in the canyon? Would that be enough shelter for you?"

"No, *jefi*," Pedro said, shaking his head.

"Good. Now," Manuel shouted, "Joaquin will unsaddle the horses and tie them to that clump of mesquite and come back. The rest of you are going to position yourselves around the canyon, and keep watch. If you get sick, vomit over the canyon. If you fall asleep and fall into the canyon, don't expect me or Miguel to pull you out. You will stay there and rot. Do you understand?"

He waited until each one nodded.

"*Bueno*. Now, move," he yelled.

Manuel laughed as the men staggered and cursed, attempting to carry out his orders. He squatted beside Miguel and rolled a cigarette.

"You were a little hard on them this morning, *amigo*," Miguel said.

"Hard on them? They are a bunch of drunken fools."

"*Sí*, but we are going to need them when we try taking the gold from Teresa and the gringo."

"You think so," Manuel said with a laugh.

"*Sí*, I think so." Miguel nodded. "Teresa knows how to shoot. She has killed men before. And don't forget Julio is riding with them. Julio Garcia is more than enough by himself. But the old gringo, Clay Best, is an army by himself. I saw him once kill four men by himself."

He turned to give Manuel a somber glance.

"The thing was, the four men had already drawn their pistols and had them pointed at Clay, when he drew his pistol and killed them all. All I am saying *amigo* is, it is not going to be easy taking the gold. You need to have some sort of plan. Just riding in and shooting will only get us all killed."

"*Sí,*" Manuel said with a thoughtful nod.

Chapter 28

Teresa and Estrella were busy making tortillas and warming left-over elk when Antonio bounded into the cave and positioned himself at the entrance with a low growl. Clay looked up from the pack he was working on to study the dog, then glanced at Julio.

"We've got company."

"*Sí.*" The vaquero pulled and cocked his pistol as he followed Clay to the greasewood by the waterfall.

"There," he said, pointing toward one dark figure near the head of the trail.

"Yeah, I see 'em. I count six or seven. There could be more."

Clay sat back to study Julio a few seconds. "Well, I reckon that puts a crimp in our plans to leave in broad daylight. You got any suggestions?"

"I could sneak out the small opening in the back of the cave and kill as many as I can," he said calmly.

"Yeah, reckon you could at that." Clay licked the paper on the cigarette he'd been rolling and handed it to Julio. "But one of them might get in a lucky shot and do for you, or leave us nursing a wounded pistolero. Na," he shook his head, "let's pass this one by the women and see if they've got any idees."

******

"What would happen if we left in the middle of the night?" Teresa asked as she poured more coffee.

"Well, I figure they're going to have at least one person on watch, and he's bound to see us, or hear the horses and mules. Then, we'd have to be traveling slow, and either take the wide trail that your papa built, or climb the rock and gravel at the far end of the canyon like Julio and Estrella done. We'd still be moving slow when they came, and we'd be risking breaking one of the animal's legs trying to climb outa here in the dark.

"Worst of all, we'd be a sitting target for them yahoos with a rifle in the daytime. It's always easier for those on a hill shooting down than it is for them having to shoot up."

"Then, what do we do?" Estrella asked.

"Well, we wait here until night, then do something different." Clay toasted her with his coffee. "You don't get this old without learning a few tricks."

******

Clay woke two hours before dawn and slipped out of the bedroll to stretch. He took a swig from the canteen and buckled his gun belt, then commanded Antonio to stay and keep watch. He leaned over and kissed Teresa. Her eyes fluttered open and she smiled before giving him a quick kiss.

"Be careful."

"I will. I didn't get this old being stupid."

Clay lit a lantern and followed the rope down the passageway toward the rear opening. He was fully awake now, and covered the distance in a matter of minutes. He doused the lantern and lit a candle before easing the saddle and blankets from the opening. He then wrapped the blankets around the saddle, and tied them with the rope.

Easing himself through the opening, he climbed slowly toward the canyon rim. He found a dried hunk of mesquite the size of a club about halfway up the incline, and decided to take it, thinking it might come in handy.

Reaching the top, he waited behind a greasewood to catch his breath. He could hear the men snoring loudly, and crept to the side of the bush to have a peek. They had made camp on the rim of the canyon, about fifty yards from the waterfall. Their camp was in the open, and he couldn't help but feel sorry for the fools, who must have been freezing in the cool desert breeze. He could see their horses, tied to a mesquite a hundred yards or so from the rim, with a pile of saddles. The flare of a match caught Clay's attention as someone lit a cigarette.

That must be the sentry.

He slipped silently from bush to bush, approaching slowly toward the man's back. As he came closer, it was easy to see in the soft moonlight the sentry was no more than a boy, maybe fifteen or sixteen years old. Instead of using his knife, as he first thought, Clay raised the club and brought it down on the youth's head with a thud. The young man rolled silently from the rock to the ground.

Clay then made his way to their horses. He took his knife and cut the cinches on each saddle before untying the lead rope. Then he took the reins of two horses and led them behind a clump of mesquite near the trail. He only had to wait seconds before the rest of the horses followed. Clay pointed the lead horses toward the trail to town and gave them each a sound swat on the rump. He then ducked back over the canyon rim as the animals galloped gladly back toward town, with a clatter of hooves against hard-packed ground and rock.

Chapter 29

Manuel was awakened by the sound of running horses, and jumped to his feet. The horses were nowhere in sight. Shouting, he pulled on his boots and grabbed his gunbelt.

"Get up! Get up, you lazy bastards!" Kicking Joaquin, he cursed and ranted as the men crawled out of their bedrolls.

"What happened?" Miguel asked, joining his side.

"What happened? What does it look like happened?" He shook one of the branches on the mesquite. "That drunken son of a whore didn't tie the horses, and now they are gone."

Manuel pulled his pistol and shot Joaquin before Miguel could stop him.

"And that fool you posted on watch never said a word or tried to stop them. Where is he?" Manuel screamed. I'm going to kill him too."

"No, Miguel said. You killed Joaquin for nothing, *amigo*." Manuel said. "Look ..." he lifted one of the saddles to show him. "Horses do not cut cinches."

"How many have been cut?" Manuel ran a hand across his face.

"All eleven." Miguel dropped the saddle as two men half-drug Andren Melozo toward them. The youth was only semi-conscious with a trickle of blood running down on his cheek. "Neither do they knock guards on the head."

"So, you claimed you were man enough to ride with Manuel Rosales. But I say you are still a boy, and not man enough to ride with us. You fell asleep at your post. Didn't you?"

"No, *señor*, I swear I didn't," Andren said weakly. "I was awake, but someone hit my head from behind."

"Too bad they didn't take your head off. You should have been watching."

Manuel turned his back on the youth and shouted.

"Everybody get ropes and find the horses! Now! Before I kill all of you."

The men scattered to look for the horses. Pedro returned half an hour later and said something to Miguel, who laughed and patted the young man on the back before ambling toward Manuel. Manuel looked up from the bottle of tequila he was nursing and snorted.

"So, what did that son of a dog say?"

"Pedro said the horses left plenty of tracks, and are headed back to the village. I think they wanted the comfort of the stable." Miguel dug a couple of cigars from his vest pocket and handed one to Manuel. "We should go get them before the gringo and Teresa leave. Even carrying the gold, they will travel faster and farther than we will on foot."

"No!" Manuel yelled, and shook his head. "You tell those idiots who lost the horses, they can go find them and bring me my horse right here." He finished by pointing toward the ground.

"Okay, *jefe*, but it will take time to get the saddles fixed. Do you want to wait out here all that time? I don't think I would. We should wait in town and eat a hot meal.

Manuel reluctantly got to his feet and cursed at the men who were still searching for horses. Shoving the bottle into his coat pocket, he picked up his saddle.

"Well, lets go. And you," he pointed a finger at Pedro, "can tell those sons of pigs I will shoot anyone who gets drunk. I want them ready to ride in the morning."

"*Sí*, but what about Andren?" Pedro said, staring at the youth. "I don't think he is ready to walk back to the village."

"Too bad," Manuel said. "If he cannot get his own horse and ride, he gets left behind. And he'll get no share of the money when we get it."

They left Andren leaning against a rock and walked back toward the village. The boy tried several times to get to his feet, and he was able to pick up his saddle one time before falling. He lay in the dirt moaning as flies started buzzing around the swollen wound on his head.

Chapter 30

Leo Santiago waited until Manuel and Miguel were well out of sight before emerging from his hiding place in the boulders. He had witnessed the entire scene. His horse had snorted and stamped his feet well before daybreak, and after quieting the animal, Leo peeked out in time to see a dark figure conk the lookout on his head with a club. The shadow then moved toward the horses picketed not twenty yards from his hiding spot, and in the moonlight, Leo was able to see it was Clay Best. After releasing the horses and sabotaging the saddles, Clay disappeared into the blackness, leading two of the horses. The rest of the horses followed seconds later.

Leo sat back contemplating what he had just seen. The fact that Clay had not come nor returned using the game trail near the waterfall meant he had found another way. Leo considered he would have to be more vigilant in watching, or he might miss seeing them when they left.

He was still considering things when a clatter of hooves against hard ground caused Manuel to leap to his feet cursing. The bandit ran to the mesquite where the horses had been tied, then started screaming at his men. It wasn't but seconds later that he shot Joaquin.

After they had gone, Leo came from his hiding place leading his horse. He stooped to check on Joaquin, only to discover the man was really dead.

"Too bad, old friend," Leo said. "I told you Manuel was not to be trusted. He is crazy and getting crazier. He will kill everyone before this is finished."

He went through Joaquin's pockets and found two hundred dollars as well as a pouch of tobacco. He stuffed the items in his vest pockets and put Joaquin's pistol in his belt. Leading his horse to where Andren lay, he knelt to check on his wound. The boy had blacked out again.

"I think Clay hit you a lot harder than he intended," he said, washing the blood from his matted hair. "But you are lucky he didn't kill you."

Leo cleaned the wound as good as he could, then helped him onto his horse. Then he tied both Andren's and Joaquin's saddles on his horse, and started the two-mile walk back to the village.

"Hold on tight, my friend. You do not want to fall from where you sit. Poco is a large horse, and you will add to the lump *Señor* Best gave you. I told you that old man was a mean one."

He paused to make sure Andren was secure, then continued toward the village.

******

Leo left Andren at *Señora* Rohas' *casa*, then gave Joaquin's saddle to the man who ran the stable as payment for caring for Andren's horse. He was surprised to find Manuel's horse, as well as those of the rest of his men. Leo left his horse tied in front of *Señora* Rohas' and walked slowly down the main road in the village, peeking into each cantina and restaurant. It was the third place he looked, a dirty flea-trap of a place called *Las Palmas*, that he saw them seated at several tables, gorging their faces and washing the food down with mugs of *cerveza*.

Leo grinned and turned back to *Señora* Rohas' *casa*. He gave the old woman twenty dollars and kissed her cheek.

"I have to go help my friends, *señora*. Please take care of this boy, and make sure he doesn't follow after those men, or he might die next time."

"*Sí Señor* Santiago, I'll get my granddaughter to help take care of the boy." The old woman hobbled excitedly toward the small adobe next door, as Leo leaned over the pallet of blankets and straw and grinned at Andren who was now awake.

"You stay here and get well, my friend. I know you only came hoping to get money to help your family. But following Manuel will get you killed. Here," Leo stuffed a hundred and twenty dollars into Andren's coat pocket, "when you get well, take that home to your mother. It is far more than you'll ever get following Manuel."

"But, *Señor* Leo. That is your money," Andren protested.

"No, it is money I found. I did not work for it, and I did not steal it. I am giving it to you, hoping it will save your life. Get well and go home. Go to church and confess to the priest. Ask *Dios* what you should do."

He grabbed Andren's hand and gave it a squeeze.

"I must go, but remember what I said. *Bueno?*"

"*Sí*, I will go," Andren said weakly.

Leo was met by the old woman and a pretty young girl he guessed to be around twelve years old as he exited the *casa*.

"Oh, *Señor* Santiago, this is my granddaughter, Maria. She will help take care of the young man."

"*Bien*," Leo said with a nod. "I must go now, but I will ask God to bless you for your kindness, *señora*."

He kissed her hand and bowed to the young girl, then left the village by circling the small adobe and using the buildings as cover. He smiled, remembering how pretty the young girl was.

"Andren may never return home. Eh, Amigo? But the maiden is pretty." He nudged the horse into a gentle lope, feeling good about himself. Perhaps helping Andren Meloza would erase some of the bad things he had done in the past, and balance the eternal scales in his favor.

Chapter 31

"Hold on, it's me," Clay called out before stepping into the main cavern. He held the lantern high and stopped as he faced two pistols and the shotgun.

"Oh," Teresa said as she rushed into his arms and kissed him.

"Huh," he said, holding her tight. "I just might have to sneak off more often."

"We hear a gunshot, and are afraid you are hurt," Estrella said, lowering the shotgun.

"Not this time. I figure it was Manuel killing one of his own men. How about some coffee? Clay said.

"Is that all you can say," Teresa snapped. "You want coffee after frightening us to death? Puh - !" She turned her back on him. "Get your own coffee!"

Clay reached for his mug but stopped as Teresa burst into tears.

"Here," he said, pulling her close to him. He held her tightly as she sobbed against his chest. She seemed to quiet after a minute and kissed him quickly on the lips.

Clay stared at the woman as she poured the coffee, then sat on a rock to study her some more. Julio offered no help. The *vaquero* simply raised his eyebrows and shrugged.

"So, tell us what happened," Teresa said after a minute.

"There's not much to tell. I slipped up behind the sentry and bonked him on the head with a hunk of wood. Then I cut the cinches on their saddles and let the horses loose. I reckon it was Manuel who was hollering when I slipped back into the hole. I heard the shot and figured he musta gone nuts and killed one of his own men."

"How many are left?" Julio asked.

"Hmm, hard to tell, but I figure, not counting the one I bonked and whoever got shot, maybe eight. Of course, it depends on how big a headache I gave the sentry, and what shape the gunshot victim is."

"Did you see Leo?" Teresa asked.

"No, but I figure he's out there, watching. He'll be around when the ball opens. I'm just wondering whose side he'll be on when the shooting starts."

"Then we must be going," Teresa said, jumping to her feet.

"Not until we're sure they've gone." Clay turned toward Julio. "Think you can sneak out the back door and let us know when it's safe to leave?"

"*Sí,*" he said with a nod. Taking the lantern, Julio disappeared quickly down the passage.

"When he gets back, we'll head out across the level valley and take the bigger trail out of here. I want to get as much space between us and that bunch of cutthroats as possible."

"*Bien,*" Teresa said as she started to pack.

Chapter 32

Manuel Rosales' head pounded with the movement of the horse. He cursed himself for having too much to drink. It had taken the rest of the day for the old saddle-maker to repair the cinches, so he had allowed Miguel to talk him into spending the night and getting an early start the following morning.

"They will be traveling slow, *amigo*, so we will catch them in the open before they reach the *Rio Grande*."

It sounded reasonable at the time, so he had agreed. Now, knowing they were at least one day behind, Manuel Rosales was in a terrible mood. He studied the green valley floor from horseback, not seeing a sign of any human life anywhere. He cursed his foolish decision not to start when the last saddle was finished. His attention was quickly diverted when one of the men yelled out and waved his arms.

"Pedro says he has found their tracks," Miguel said as he approached.

Manuel leaned in the saddle to study the hoof marks at the head of the wide trail.

"*Sí*," Pedro said excitedly. "Four horses carrying men. Two heavy and two light. And there are two mules, very heavy."

"So, they did find the gold," Manuel said thoughtfully. He grinned and leaned to clasp Pedro's arm. "See? Here's a real man I can count on," he said loudly. "He has found the gringo and the gold. *Bueno*," he said to the *pistolero*. "You will have Joaquin's share as well as your own."

They followed Clay and Teresa's trail south, following the canyon. Miguel voiced his concern that they had taken little, if any, effort to hide their tracks.

"And how are they going to hide their tracks, eh?" Manuel mocked him. "They have heavy mules, and nothing to cover the tracks with."

He urged his men into a fast gallop. "I can smell the gold!" he yelled. The canyon turned into a dry arroyo, containing boulders and brush. Then, as if by magic, the tracks disappeared.

"What the hell happened? Where are they?" He dismounted and grabbed Pedro by the shoulders, shaking the man. "You found them. Now, tell me where they went."

"I don't know, *jefe*." Pedro pleaded.

"Then find them before I kill you." He drew his gun, but Miguel grabbed his arm.

"Whoa, hold on, my friend. We will need every gun we have once we face Julio and the gringo. *Bueno?*"

"*Bueno*," Manuel said with a nod.

It took about fifteen minutes before Poco found the spot where Clay had entered the arroyo. The bandits reached the bottom of the wash in a cloud of dust, then Manuel ordered Poco and Pedro to find their trail. The men led their horses downstream until Pedro shouted.

"See, *jefe*? Here they are. We are going in the right direction.

"So, they are trying to stay out of sight by following the arroyo, eh? But they still head for Texas. *Bueno*, we will go to Texas also. Quickly, to the top," Manuel yelled as he spurred his horse back up the sandy bank. "We will ride quickly and trap them inside the arroyo."

Chapter 33

Julio had returned about twenty minutes later, carrying the saddle and blankets.

"They have gone, *Señor* Clay. I watched them walk toward town, then I see Leo take a young boy on his horse. I think the boy's head was badly hurt."

"That must've been the one I bonked on the noggin," Clay said thoughtfully. "I didn't mean to hit him that hard, but anyone out to take something that doesn't belong to them can expect to get hurt. Anything else?"

"*Sí,*" he said with a nod. "I found Joaquin on the ground. He had been shot in the chest."

"Hmm, that makes Manuel a dangerous fellow to work for," Clay said with a snort. "Well, I reckon we'd best get moving and try to put a little daylight between us and them. Then...."

Both men paused and stared at the cave opening at the now familiar sound of Teresa vomiting.

"Good God in heaven," Clay said and heaved a deep sigh. "I wonder what's wrong with her?"

"I don't know, *señor*. Maybe she should see the doctor when we get to Carrizo Springs."

"You can bet she is, even if I have to force her."

******

They exited the cave and followed the game trail to the floor of the canyon. Teresa crossed herself in prayer as they passed the burnt-out hull of her parent's house. Minutes later, they were climbing the trail toward the rim of the canyon.

With the animals rested and well fed, they made excellent time on the flat ground near the canyon rim. Soon, the green grass and water disappeared into a tangle of gravel and rocks as the pretty homestead turned into a dry arroyo with brush and cactus. They followed the arroyo for several miles before Estrella galloped to the front.

"Here is where my family stays," she said, pointing toward a large hill of rock and boulders.

"Were?" Clay asked.

"Inside the hill," Julio said, shaking his head. "I did not believe it either, but the hill is hollow, and they have water."

"That makes for a nice hideout. But we'd better keep moving and not attract attention to your folks," Clay said, and turned his horse south.

They kept moving at a steady walk for another hour before Clay stopped.

"You say this here wash heads all the way to the Rio Grande?"

"*Sí*, that is what my uncle says," Estrella said.

"Well, let's make use of it," He said and turned his horse down the sandy bank. He waited until they had reached the bottom, then called a break.

Teresa unwrapped a pack of tortillas she had cooked in the cave and passed them around. Clay took a swallow from a canteen and studied Estrella's somber face.

"I know you wanted to see your folks. But if we stopped to swap howdies, and them following us showed up, some of your folks would've gotten hurt. You and Julio can come back later for a visit."

"*Sí*," she said with a nod and smiled.

"From now on, we'd best make good time. I recollect chasing a couple of rustlers into a wash south of the Rio when I was working for Les Bishop. If it's the same wash, I figure we'll reach the Rio Grande day after tomorrow, and the Cool Water Ranch. From there, it's only ten miles into Carrizo Springs. Manuel and his gang of thieves won't bother us there."

"*Sí*," Teresa said with a nod. "How far ahead are we, now?"

"Not far enough," Clay said with a laugh. "I think we might have a ten to fifteen mile lead by the end of the day. We could get twenty miles, but I doubt it. We can't run the mules without killing them, that's for sure."

They rested the animals for a half an hour before starting again. Clay and Julio cut brush to drag behind their horses in a effort to erase their tracks.

That night they made a dry, dark camp, not wanting to risk a fire that would attract Manuel or Indians. They rose and saddled the animals quietly in the cool pre-dawn air, and had covered several miles before the heat of the sun began to slow the mules.

"Come on, you cursed varmints," Clay said, swatting one of them on the rump. "It's hot on us all. Show us what a genuine Tennessee plow mule is made of."

He called another break at noon to rest the animals, and give them water from one of the water bags. Teresa and Estrella found a shady spot near a boulder and closed their eyes, while Clay and Julio took turns keeping watch.

They were moving an hour later, and by mid-afternoon, Clay was beginning to think they might've given Manuel the slip. The floor of the arroyo took on a slight downward slope toward the river, making it easier on the mules. They rounded a bend in the arroyo and were met by several Indians.

"Dear God in heaven," Clay said, heaving a sigh. Estrella smiled and trotted her pony forward and began a conversation with the leader.

"Family?" Clay asked.

"*Sí*," Julio said with a nod.

"Well, that's good. I figured I might've lost my hair for a minute."

Clay dismounted and took several sticks of jerked beef from his saddlebag and passed them to the Indians. Estrella continued the conversation for a few minutes longer, then, without warning, the Indians galloped away.

"What did they want?" Teresa asked as Estrella dismounted.

"He say we have this many men following us." She held up eight fingers. "He says they are not good men, and to be careful."

"Manuel," Clay said with a growl. "Did he say how far back they are?

"He says one, maybe two hours behind. They are up on high ground," she pointed toward the bank of the arroyo, "and they are moving fast."

"Well, we sure can't out run them," Clay said as Teresa grabbed his hand. "Besides, I don't know how everyone else is feeling about this game, but I'm getting tired of them woolin' us around."

"*Bien*," Julio said with a nod. He pulled his pistol and started checking the loads. "We go get them now?"

"Na, I don't want a fire-fight with eight in broad daylight. Besides, we'd have to abandoned the mules and the gold if we did."

He popped the cork on one of the canteens and took a swig, then passed it to Teresa.

"I vote that we make camp right here and let 'em catch up to us. The difference is, we're gonna be expecting them. Here's what I want each of you to do when that time comes...."

Chapter 34

Manuel sat on a small boulder in the shade of a mesquite, waiting impatiently. They had punished the horses in the heat of the day, trying to catch Teresa and the gringo before they crossed the Rio Grande. He was not opposed to crossing into Texas to rob or kill someone. He had done that many times. What he was opposed to was upsetting the gringo lawman at Carrizo Springs. He had done that once, and the man ignored the laws that say Americanos cannot chase men into Mexico. Miguel said that the gringo they were chasing used to be such a lawman, and did the same thing. That was of no concern to Manuel, since he planned to catch and kill him here in Mexico.

He looked up as Miguel approached.

"Well, what has Poco discovered?" Manuel asked.

"He said they are making camp about one half mile south, in the arroyo."

"Ha! I told you the gringo was not as smart as me." Manuel jumped to his feet laughing. "Did I not tell you? If he was smart, he would not have allowed himself to get boxed in. We shall be up on top, shooting down on them. They will be like ants, and all we have to do is step on them."

"*Sí, jefe*, it would seem that way. But be careful. I heard this man is a foxy one. He might be luring us into a trap."

"A trap? Do you think Manuel Rosales is stupid enough to get caught in a trap? Is that what you think, Miguel?" Manuel roared.

"No, I am not saying that at all. All I am saying is, I don't think the old gringo is stupid enough to get himself caught in an arroyo with two women and the gold."

Miguel lit a cigar and passed it to Manuel, then slowly lit a second for himself, allowing time for his words to sink in.

"Yes," Manuel finally said with a nod. "I see what you mean, old friend. Maybe he is an old fox who is trying to set a trap. Maybe this will be a battle between two foxes, eh Miguel?" Manuel laughed. He pulled the cork on a bottle of tequila and passed it to Miguel.

"So, here is what we are going to do, my friend." Manuel squatted to draw his plan in the dirt with his finger.

Chapter 35

They built a small campfire and spread their bedrolls close enough to the fire for the bandits to see plainly, then stuffed them with blankets to make them look like they were sleeping. Tying the mules and horses to a mesquite, they climbed out of the wash fifty yards downstream and took a position behind a large greasewood. The ground was still hot and burnt Clay's knees as he knelt. A full moon rose, casting a soft glow over the desert as a coyote gave it's lonely cry. Teresa shifted closer and kissed his ear.

"Be careful, *marido muy fuerte*. I do not like wearing the widow's veil."

"You too. I hate burying women. Especially those I'm married to."

They didn't have long to wait as one black silhouette appeared, then ran toward a pile of rocks and dropped out of sight. Julio nudged Clay's arm and pointed.

"Yeah, I saw him," Clay whispered.

"Shhh," Teresa said, calming Antonio as the dog growled.

Another silhouette appeared, running to a clump of bushes, then another and another. They continued until Clay had counted seven men. He nodded to himself, feeling satisfied that Manuel would stay put, and order his men from a safe position.

"Okay, let's open the ball," Clay whispered and cocked his pistol.

Teresa slipped into the darkness toward Clay's left, while Julio disappeared toward his right. Estrella darted toward a large boulder with Antonio at her heels. Clay inched toward another greasewood then stopped. He suddenly had a feeling that something wasn't right. He figured Manuel and his boys would be firing at the bedrolls by now, or maybe even rushing the campfire. But there wasn't a sound.

"*Dammit!*" He couldn't help feeling that he had just led them into a trap.

"Hey, gringo! I've got your woman, gringo. If you want her, you'll have to come get her. Can you hear me, gringo?"

Chapter 36

Teresa had run quietly toward the boulders and ducked into the shadows. She slipped around the boulder, inching into position. When her husband gave the word, she would begin firing at the men who had been following them. It was a good plan, and it would end the long days of trying to hide and endless nights of keeping watch.

She inched farther to the right. She was almost there when she felt the cold steel of a gun barrel against her head.

"*Buenas noches, señora.* I will take care of the pistol."

Teresa released her hold on the Smith and Wesson as he wrenched it from her hand. She gagged and fought an urge to vomit as he rubbed his unshaven face against her cheek. He smelled of a combination of stale tequila, corn tortillas.and sour sweat.

"I will take the other gun also." He pulled the other pistol from its holster.

"Now, you will do exactly as I say, or I will destroy this pretty face."

He grabbed her cheeks and jerked her face toward his to kiss her lips. Teresa spit in his face and got slapped soundly.

"That is good, *señora.*" Manuel grinned as Teresa's spit trickled down his cheek. "I like a woman to fight. It makes the victory even better. Now," he grabbed her by the hair and jerked her away from the rock, "we will let your husband watch while I have fun with you."

Manuel drug Teresa into the open, then pulled her body against his, holding her firmly with his left arm locked tightly around her throat.

"Hey gringo," he yelled. "I've got your woman, gringo. If you want her, you'll have to come get her. Can you hear me, gringo?"

Teresa caught her breath as Clay appeared behind a bush, looking pale and haggard in the moonlight.

Dios, she prayed silently. *Forgive me for being a stupid woman and getting caught. Now my husband will have to suffer because of me. Forgive me, Father, and give us victory over these evil men.*

Chapter 37

Clay felt physically ill, thinking of what might happen with Teresa in the hands of a madman. He saw her in the moonlight as she crossed herself in prayer.

Lord, I ain't never asked you for much, but since you already took June, I'd appreciate it if you'd help me kill that son-of-a-bitch and save Teresa.

He'd no more than gotten the prayer said inside his head when someone moved on the other side of the greasewood. Clay eased back a branch and saw Miguel scrunched close to the ground. The man evidently had no idea he was hiding behind the same bush, and was intent on watching Teresa squirm against Manuel's hold on her neck.

Clay rammed the muzzle of his .45 against the base of Miguel's neck and the man froze. Without being asked, Miguel passed his pistol, butt first, over his shoulder for Clay to take.

"I'm here, Manuel," Clay said loudly. "And I'd appreciate you unhanding my wife."

Manuel roared with laughter. "No, now I'll tell you what you're going to do, *gringo*. You and all your friends are going to throw your guns into a pile, or I'm going to kill your woman."

"Well," Clay chuckled, "that'd be inconvenient, since I've got my .45 pointed at your friend's head."

"What friend? I will kill her, *gringo*."

Teresa gagged as he tightened his hold.

"Come on," Clay tapped Miguel on the back of the head with his gun barrel, "let's show the man."

Miguel slowly rose with his hands raised.

"See? I wasn't fooling when I said I had your man. I found him lurking behind this bush. So, what's it going to be? How about we swap? My wife for your friend?"

Manuel roared with laughter.

"No, *gringo*, that is not how it is going to be. If Miguel is stupid enough to get caught, then you can have him. I do not like *estúpidos* working for me."

"Well, I reckon I was right when I said it would be dangerous working for you."

"*Sí*, but you and I are not *estúpidos*, are we *gringo*?"

"No, I don't reckon we are."

Clay motioned Miguel forward until he stood facing Teresa.

"So, what's it going to be, Manuel? Are we gonna kill each other, or have a Mexican standoff and spend the night jawing?"

The six remaining members of Manuel's gang had drifted back to watch the proceedings, and were standing to Clay's left. Clay could see Julio standing in the shadows on his right. He had no idea where Estrella was, but he could hear Antonio's low growl in the bushes.

"You say I'm supposed to let the woman go and face you alone?" Manuel laughed again.

"Yeah, that's exactly what I'm saying. I'll release Miguel at the same time. Then it's just you and me. What could be more fair?"

"Fair? Why should I care about fair? I've got the woman. And very soon, I'm going to kill you and have the gold also," Manuel said.

The crunching of boots against gravel caught their attention as Leo Santiago appeared out of the darkness. The man looked calm and collected as he paused to look at Manuel, then Clay, and back to Manuel.

"Manuel, Manuel, Manuel," Leo said, shaking his head. "We've been through this a dozen times, but you still don't get it, do you? There is no need to talk about killing a man. You simply do it."

He whipped his gun from the holster and swung it toward Clay and pulled the trigger.

Chapter 38

Teresa had quit struggling against Manuel's arm at her throat. Every effort had only caused him to tighten his hold, cutting off her breath. The last effort had almost caused her to pass out, so she relaxed as much as possible, taking in several gulps of air.

Then, like an answer to prayer, Leo appeared out of the darkness, looking as if he were in control. She suddenly knew what she must do, but her heart leaped in terror when Leo drew his pistol and fired. The bullet hit Miguel in the forehead.

Manuel cursed loudly, and swung his gun toward Leo, but Teresa quickly raised her foot and brought the heel of her riding boot down on his foot with all her weight. Manuel yelled and released his hold on her as the bone in his right foot snapped. She slipped to the ground and rolled out of his reach.

******

Leo knew his chance of getting Clay and Teresa out of this alive without getting himself killed was slim, but he felt he owed Clay, since the man had saved him more than once. Manuel had a tight hold on Teresa, who was struggling. Shooting him without hitting her was a chance he didn't want to risk. But, Clay was standing a couple of feet behind Miguel, holding a gun to his back. If he could get a good angle, he might be able to get a clean shot at Miguel without hitting Clay. Besides, Leo knew Miguel was a better shot than Manuel.

He walked casually toward the six men standing in the shadows, shaking his head and chiding Manuel for being stupid. When he thought he had a good angle, Leo whipped his pistol and fired, hitting Miguel in the head. He spun quickly, hoping to get a shot at Manuel, but a bullet from Pedro's gun knocked him to the ground.

******

Clay's knees almost buckled when Leo fired. The bullet snapped Miguel's head backward, showering Clay with blood. Manuel bellowed as Miguel crumpled, and Teresa hit the ground rolling. Clay fired twice, sending Manuel sprawling backward as a shot from the men in the shadows sent Leo to the ground. Clay dove for cover as all hell erupted in gunfire.

******

Estrella had been struggling to keep Antonio calm, but the big dog sensed his master was in trouble and was having none of it. She glanced down, rubbing the dog's back. The hair on his neck was bristled, and drool dripped from his bared fangs. She caught her breath and cocked both hammers on the shotgun as Leo Santiago strolled out of the darkness. The man appeared casual, as though he were visiting old friends. Then he drew his gun and shot Miguel in the head.

Estrella jerked upright as Pedro fired his pistol, knocking Leo to the ground. Antonio leaped over the bush with a snarl, landing on Pedro's chest. Pedro fell with a scream as the dog latched onto his neck, shaking and tearing his victim. One of the men cursed and aimed his pistol at the dog, but a blast from Estrella's shotgun lifted him from his feet.

******

Teresa scooped Manuel's pistol from the dust and crawled behind a large rock near a mesquite. There were five men standing, who for a few seconds, seemed transfixed at watching Antonio maul their comrade. One of the men raised his gun toward the dog and Estrella shot him. The men suddenly came alive, and fired several shots at Estrella, but the girl had disappeared behind a boulder. Teresa fired three times, hitting one of the men in his mid-section. He staggered several steps before collapsing.

******

The remaining four men crowded behind a large boulder, firing wild shots toward Teresa as she scrunched closer to the rock behind the mesquite. Julio took aim as one of the men fired. He waited as the man ducked behind the rock, then fired as the head came back up. The man pitched backward with a bullet in his forehead.

******

Clay motioned toward Julio to circle toward the right, and then slipped from bush to rock and more bushes as he circled toward the left. The remaining men fired randomly, and Clay grinned as Teresa responded with several shots of her own.

Clay reached the bush where Estrella was hiding and patted her on the back as she grinned at him.

"I want you to fire at the rock they're behind when I start moving. Okay?"

She nodded.

"Just be careful. Julio is somewhere on the other side. With any luck, we'll finish this now."

Clay waited a few seconds to study the situation. Julio appeared, crawling behind a bush on the opposite side of the boulder. Clay gave him a *stay low* sign and pointed out his position to Estrella. He waited a few more seconds before patting Estrella on the back.

"Now!" he said, and ran toward the rock. The shotgun boomed once, then twice as Clay dove under a greasewood. One of the men had raised to shoot at the girl, but jerked back as Clay hit the dirt. He fired at Clay and missed. Clay's first shot hit him in the hip. He fell, then raised his gun once more before Clay shot him.

The last two men chose to shoot as they ran for the horses. Three well placed shots from Julio sent one of them to the ground as Clay ended the battle with a shot that took the last man between the shoulders.

Clay leaned against a boulder quietly reloading his gun and thanking God for hearing his prayer. He finally took a deep breath a yelled.

"How is everyone? Teresa? Are you okay?"

"*Bueno*, my love."

"Julio?"

"*Sí*, all is well."

"Estrella? You alright, girl?

"*Sí*, I am fine."

The nearness of the girl's voice made him jump. He turned to find her standing beside him.

"Ha," he laughed. "I started to say you're as quiet as an Indian, but I guess you really are."

The sound of pounding hooves brought him to his feet. He ran to where Manuel had been lying and stared at the blood-stained dirt.

"Manuel! How in the hell..." Clay shouted. He turned toward Julio who was standing beside him.

"I shot him....twice."

"*Sí*, but he still lives," Julio said.

"I thought he was dead," Teresa said. "I have his gun." She held the Colt for everyone to see.

"Dammit! I should've shot him again, in the head."

"*Señor* Clay, there were too many bullets," Estrella said, shaking her head. "You would have been shot."

"Maybe we'll still get shot, with him on the loose."

Teresa knelt beside Leo and placed a hand on his chest.

"Leo is still alive, but hurt badly," she said. "Estrella go to the horses and bring the medical supplies."

Clay knelt beside the man as Teresa unbuttoned his shirt.

"That was a damned fool thing you did, Leo. What made you do it? I thought you was smarter than that."

"It was the only way I could think of to save you and *Señora* Best," Leo said through clenched teeth. "Oh, it hurts."

"Well, that's something a .45 is supposed to do," Clay said with a snort. "Just remember, I didn't ask you to do it. You did it on your own. Besides, I ain't quite decided who's side you're really on. You could've been trying to plug me and hit Miguel by mistake."

"Hush your talk," Teresa said, giving him a cold glare. "He got hurt trying to save us."

Estrella returned with a lantern and carrying a bag with the bandages and medicine. Clay glanced up at Julio as the *vaquero* calmly rolled a cigarette.

"Why don't you and Estrella take a look around and see if there's anyone lurking in the dark? We'll be done here in a few minutes."

"I said, he's badly hurt," Teresa hissed. "This may take some time."

"It'd better not take too long. We're going to have to get moving first thing in the morning."

"He is right, *señora*," Leo said weakly. "You can leave me. Just take care of my wife and little boy."

"You've got to be joking," Clay boomed. "If you think I'm gonna saddle myself with taking care of your family, you've got another think coming. You didn't do all that much."

"*Sí*, we will send for them," Teresa said sweetly before giving Clay a warning glare.

"Oh, for the life of me, I wished we would've stayed in Carrizo Springs," Clay growled. He fetched a bottle of tequila from the medical kit and pulled the cork, then poured a generous amount on Leo's wound and grinned as Leo yelled in pain, then took a sip.

"*Bruta*," Teresa said, snatching the bottle from his lips. She held the bottle for Leo to sip, then recorked it and put it back in the bag. "We shall take him with us, and if he dies, we will take care of his family. There will be no more discussions on the matter. *Bueno*?"

"Yeah, I understand what you're saying, but I ain't playing no nursemaid to a cry-baby who ain't got no more of a hurt than that," he said, pointing toward the wound high in Leo's chest and near his collar bone. "I've had worser wounds than that, and was still able to fork a horse and take myself to the doctor.

He stood as Julio and Estrella returned with the same group of Indians Estrella had claimed for her family. The leader said something and Estrella interpreted.

"He says to congratulate you on a great victory."

"Tell him he's welcome," Clay said with a nod, then mumbled low to himself, "Although we could've used a little help."

"He also says they will take those men's horses and guns," Estrella said.

"I reckon that will be alright, seeing as we can't handle any more," Clay said.

"He also says they saw a group of Mexican Federales this afternoon. They are about two miles south."

"Figures." Clay heaved a deep sigh. "What else?"

Estrella spoke rapidly, then interrupted.

"He thinks the Federales are looking for a band of Apaches who raided a small rancho. He says they will have heard the gunshots, and will be coming to see what happened. He says we should leave before they get here."

"Sounds like good advice. Tell him I said thank you."

Clay turned toward Teresa with his hands on his hips.

"You heard what she said. We've got three options. You and Estrella can pack his wound and help him onto his horse while Julio and me pack the mules, and then get moving. If we're lucky, we just might make it to the Rio Grande before they catch us. Or we can forget the mules and gold and make a run for it. We'd stand a better chance of out-running those soldiers, moving light. Or, we can just leave him here for the Federales. You call it. What do you want to do?"

"We will take Leo and the gold and beat them to the *rio*," Teresa said firmly.

Okay, let's get 'er done," Clay said. He started to leave, then stopped to glare at Leo.

"Two things. First of all, where in the hell's your horse? I ain't carrying you double."

"Amigo is behind the rocks and brush that way," he said, pointing with his left hand.

"Estrella, ..." Clay started, but the girl was already running toward the brush.

"What is the other thing?" Leo asked.

"You'd better ride this bronc out, 'cause I don't want to spend what time I've got left bustin' rocks in some Mexican prison, and I sure as hell don't want to see my wife wearing prison garb. Understand?"

"*Sí*, I will not slow you down."

Chapter 39

Captain Jose Ramos of the fifth regiment of Los Federales de Mexicanos had ordered his men to make camp one hour before sunset. They had been commissioned out of Fort Conchos to investigate reports of a band of renegade Apaches that had been raiding farms. It was suspected the Indians were systematically hitting the small farms and ranchos on their way toward Texas, and they would likely do the same on their return back into Mexico.

"Gracias," he said, accepting the tin plate filled with rice and beans, and a cup of coffee from Lieutenant Raoul Flores. It was all about to change in a matter of days. Jose would be retiring when they returned to the fort, and Raoul would be taking command of the regiment. He took a deep breath and exhaled slowly.

"Ah, I shall miss this, Lieutenant Flores. There is nothing like the fresh desert air."

"I suppose not, Captain," Raoul said with a grin. "The desert air is all I've known."

"Oh, I forgot," Jose said, turning Raoul toward the young Lieutenant. "You've never been to Mexico City, have you?"

"No," he said, shaking his head.

"You need to go and see it, at least once. Promise me you will, on your next leave. Then, you can return to your post and enjoy the desert."

"Is it really that ugly?" Lieutenant Flores asked with a grin.

"Ugly? No, no," Jose said with a laugh. "Mexico City is quite beautiful. But it is too crowded. I didn't know there were that many people in the world, until I saw Mexico City. Then, I couldn't wait to return to the desert."

"What will you do when you retire?"

"Juanita and I plan to return to the family farm near Juarez and enjoy our grandchildren."

They paused at the sound of a gunshot. It was distant, but sound carried well in the desert with the lack of distracting noise.

"Quiet!" Jose yelled.

Almost as if on cue, several more shots rang out, followed by what must have certainly been a full-blown battle. Then, nothing but silence.

"What do you think it is, Captain?" Lieutenant Flores asked.

"I think it is another sleepless night with no food, Lieutenant. "That is what I think." He scraped the beans and rice onto the ground and passed the empty plate to the Lieutenant, then turned to the men.

"You all heard the gunshots. Break camp and get mounted. Check all weapons. It could be the Apaches we are seeking, or it could be something else. What it most certainly is, is trouble. I want you ready in ten minutes."

He turned to grin at his Lieutenant.

"Finish your coffee, my friend. It will be the last you'll have tonight.

Chapter 40

Teresa and Estrella packed Leo's wound with sulfur powder, herbs and dried cactus pulp, then wrapped him tightly with strips of cloth. Clay and Julio had the mules packed and horses saddled by the time they had finished. They helped Leo onto his horse, then mounted their own. Clay trotted Loco toward Leo and nodded.

"You ready to burn some leather?"

"*Sí*," he said with a nod.

"Okay, remember what I said. If you can't keep up, I'm leaving you as buzzard bait."

"*Bueno.*"

"Let's ride," Clay said loudly, and nudged Loco in the flanks. The caravan moved down the wash until they found a safe spot to climb back to the desert floor. They hadn't gone a quarter of a mile before Teresa trotted Diablo up beside Clay and glared at him.

"You will not leave Leo lying in the desert. Do you understand?"

"Well, I reckon you'd rather be caught by the Federales? Is that what you want?"

"No, but you are not leaving him," she snapped.

"No, I don't guess you'd let me live in peace if I left him, would you?" Clay snorted and guided Loco around a clump of cactus.

"If he falls out of the saddle, I'll tie him on his horse. How's that?"

"*Bien*," she said with a nod.

They moved through the night, following the wash in the moonlight. Clay and Julio took turns, either dropping back to see if they were being followed, or riding forward to see what lay ahead. They had covered ten miles by the time the sun began to peek over the horizon.

"I reckon this might be a good time to rest the mules and check on our friend," Clay said. "He seems to be sagging a little in the saddle."

Clay and Julio helped Leo from the horse and laid him on a sandy area.

"Better ride back a ways and see if anyone's on our tail," he said to Julio. "I'll scout up ahead a ways and do the same."

"*Bien*," Julio said with a nod.

Clay watched him ride away, then climbed back on Loco. He paused to look at Teresa and Estrella as they repacked Leo's wound.

"Think you can have him ready to ride in half an hour?"

"*Sí*, I will try," Teresa said.

"There ain't no trying to it. We'd better cross that river ahead of the Federales, or we likely won't see Texas again."

"*Sí*," Teresa said with a nod. "He will be ready."

She looked Leo in the eyes as Clay rode away.

"You'll have to excuse my husband. I can tell he is worried, and afraid we will be caught. You will have to stay on your horse and ride with the rest of us. *Bien*?"

"*Bien, Señora* Best. You're husband is right. You don't want to get caught by the Federales trying to cross the river with Mexican gold. They will not listen or care how you found it." Leo grinned. "*Gracias, señora*, I shall not let you down."

Chapter 41

Captain Ramos dismounted to study the battle scene in the red glow of the sunrise. It had taken longer than anticipated to find the spot in the dark. Now, staring at the scattered bodies, he found a strange humor in what he was looking at.

"*El capitán*, isn't this one Miguel Villa?"

"*Sí, el teniente*," Captain Ramos said with a nod. "That is Miguel Villa. But there is one missing?"

"Missing?"

"*Sí*, over here." Captain Ramos pointed toward the blood-stained earth. "There is quite a bit of blood, and the sign of a struggle for life, but no body."

He turned to follow a trail of blood to a spot where several horses had been tied.

"One of them got away, even though he was severely wounded."

"I wonder if he went to the village?" Lieutenant Flores asked.

"Probably," Captain Ramos said with a nod. "It is the closest place to seek help. Have a couple of men go to the village and knock on every door. Have them check and see if anyone has encountered a gunshot victim, then report back to us."

"*Sí, capitán*." He turned to go, but stopped at Ramos' voice.

"And Lieutenant, tell them if we are not here, they are to follow our tracks to the Rio Grande."

"Rio Grande, *capitán*?"

"*Sí*, that is the way the victors headed."

He waited while the Lieutenant carried out the orders, then laughed, shaking his head.

"Do you see humor in this carnage, Captain?" Lieutenant Flores asked.

"Humor? No, simply irony. It would seem that someone has done us a great favor." He looked around once more and chuckled. "I guess I should be angry, Lieutenant, but I also feel I should shake the hands of those who made our job easier."

"Juan says it was Indians. See the moccasin prints? There are more over here. He says maybe Yaqui."

"No, Indians didn't do this. Come here, and I will show you," he said, placing a hand on the Lieutenant's shoulder. "First, you can see where they reloaded their weapons and left the empty cartridges. Everyone but two men were killed with pistols. I do know that some Indians use pistols, but very few. One man was mauled by a dog, and the other was killed with a shotgun, in what looks like a Texas-style gun battle.

"No," he added, shaking his head. "I believe the Indians came later and took guns and horses, but they did not kill these men."

"Then, who did?"

"Ah, now that is the question you are going to have to answer. Once you take command, these are the very things you will face. To solve the puzzle, you need to study every detail and judge things carefully. Watch, and I'll show you what you must do."

Captain Ramos turned to Sergeant Villa.

"Sergeant, I need you to take your pad and draw a diagram of this mess. Put in every detail that you can."

"*Bien, el capitán*." The sergeant pulled a sketch pad with a quill and bottle of ink from his saddle bag and climbed on a rock for a better view as he began to draw.

"Privates Torres and Ortiz, you will stay with Sergeant Villa until he is finished, then you will escort him north, following the arroyo, and join us at the Rio Grande."

"*Bien, el capitán*," they replied with a snappy salute.

"You mentioned the Rio Grande before, Captain." Lieutenant Flores said. "What makes you think whoever it was is heading toward the Rio Grande?"

"Wouldn't you, Lieutenant, if you had just killed seven men, and wounded an eighth? I imagine they are carrying something of value that maybe doesn't belong to them, and they would rather not get caught."

Captain Ramos grinned at the puzzled look on the Lieutenant's face.

"Come, Lieutenant, let me ask you. I know you have heard of Miguel Villa before, haven't you?"

"*Sí*," he said with a nod.

"Miguel Villa never traveled far without the company of Manuel Rosales. And, I'm sure you know them to be cold-blooded killers. Am I right?"

"Yes, they have killed several men."

"Good. Now, ask yourself. When they killed people, what else did they do?"

"They robbed them?"

"*Sí*, now we are getting somewhere. I don't think Miguel Villa died by accident. No, he was after whatever these men are carrying. And when they tried to rob them, they met more than their match. Now, the question is, what do their killers have worth dying for?"

"Maybe the missing gold General Bernal took?" Lieutenant Flores asked with a hint of excitement.

"Now, you are thinking like a leader, Lieutenant. Our job is to find them and see if you are right.

"Do you think the wounded one who got away is Manuel Rosales?"

"Most likely. Have the men mount their horses."

Lieutenant Flores gave the order, and they mounted in unison.

"*Perdóname, el capitán*," Lieutenant Flores said as the regiment began to move forward. "What about the bodies?"

"Well now, that does pose a problem, doesn't it? I would like to take them with us, but we do not have the spare horses. And I know that protocol would say that we bury them, but digging eight graves in this rocky soil would take precious time, during which, the men we are chasing might cross the Rio Grande and enter America."

"So, we will leave them?"

"*Sí*, Lieutenant. I don't think they are going anywhere. We shall bury them, or what's left of them, when we return."

Chapter 42

Manuel Rosales had thought briefly of snatching his pistol from the dirt and shooting the old gringo. But he was wounded and losing blood fast. Then, Teresa grabbed his pistol and crawled quickly behind a rock, leaving him with little else than to lie in the dirt bleeding. If he moved, he would likely get shot again.

The gringo had fired twice, with the first bullet hitting him in the left shoulder, and the second burning a path across his chest as he pitched backward. He considered himself lucky.

The entire battle lasted no more than a minute, and when he heard the gringo shouting Teresa's name, he knew the *estúpido* men he had been stuck with were dead. Teresa scrambled to her feet and ran toward the gringo and Indian girl, leaving him with a slim chance of escaping. Manuel rolled to his hands and knees, and snatching Leo's pistol from the dirt, he slipped into the bushes and grabbed the first horse he could find. It was Miguel's appaloosa.

Somehow, he pulled himself into the saddle and dug his heels into the animal's flanks, then hung onto the pommel with both hands. The horse darted forward with a clatter of hooves and shouts from those left behind.

The appaloosa hit the trail to the village and broke into a full run. Manuel felt light-headed and leaned into the horse's neck. He was ready to black out when he spied the tiny farmhouse, and guided the lathered beast to the front door. He fell from the saddle as the old peon came from the tiny *casa*. Manuel couldn't remember much after that. Only that someone helped the old man carry him inside, and poured a generous amount of brandy down his throat.

Chapter 43

Lester Bishop sat in his favorite chair inside the dirty saloon. His hand shook as he poured another drink, and the neck of the bottle rattled against the grimy glass on the table. Cobwebs hung like silver threads from the beams on the ceiling and danced in the breeze from the open windows. The dirty dance floor was a sad reminder of the grandeur that had once belonged to The Cool Water Saloon. A year earlier, the dance floor had been crowded with laughing cowhands and dancing girls in skimpy clothing. Each table had a different card game going and the beer and whiskey flowed like water. Best of all, it belonged to him...the entire town.

In reality, Cool Water, Texas couldn't be called a town by any stretch of the imagination. In fact, it wasn't a town at all, but consisted of a few houses and *jacales* scattered haphazardly on the Texas plain, with one small general store, a combination blacksmith and livery stable, a fair-sized saloon and dance hall with a brothel, one small bank and an even smaller church. The name *Cool Water* had been taken from Lester Bishop's ranch, *Cool Water Cattle Ranch.* Lester had discovered the natural springs while buying cattle in Piedrao Negras, Mexico and promptly bought the land, one thousand acres of it, and built his ranch.

After a heated argument with some bankers in San Antonio, Lester decided to build his own bank and city, and plans were drawn, subdividing the town-site. Then he began negotiating with the International Great-Northern Railroad to build a spur to his ranch. Believing middle managment personnel were beneath him, Lester went to Chicago and finagled a meeting with the chairman of the board. The man listened politely, then promptly refused him, as San Antonio already had three railroads, and two others scheduled for the near future.

"Building a spur to your ranch doesn't make financial sense, Mr. Bishop. We would only be hauling cattle from your ranch, and perhaps small amounts of goods to and from Carrizo Springs, if we chose to build a depot there…which is not likely. Besides, it's only what, sixty or seventy miles from your ranch to San Antonio? Seventy, or even a hundred miles isn't much of a cattle drive for a Texan."

"Look," he said when Lester began to argue, "build your town, and if you can prove there would be enough profit…enough passengers, cattle and goods to make it feasible…I'll personally push the idea."

The idea never took hold, no matter how much effort and money Lester Bishop invested. Marauding Indians and bandits plagued the area, killing settlers, and making off with his cattle. Five years and thousands of dollars later, Cool Water, Texas was not even a recognized town-site, other than in Lester Bishop's mind. His four successes, which he gloried in, were the store, where the people living on his ranch and the surrounding area bought goods at inflated prices; the saloon and dance hall, where his cowboys spent their hard-earned money on cheap liquor and even cheaper whores who gave Lester a cut of their profits; his granddaughter, Ruth, who he thought was the loveliest girl in Texas and who he thought no one of a lesser social status than himself worthy of marrying; and his bank, but not necessarily in that order. If the truth were known, the bank was his crowning achievement, since it had never been robbed, and kept his ever-growing stash of money safe and sound.

Then, there was the hiring of Clay Best as town marshal. Clay had been a well-known lawman when Lester happened to meet him in San Antonio while trying to negotiate with the railroad. Clay's wife, June, was seriously ill, and he was considering resigning his post with plans to move to the cleaner and less populated high deserts of Arizona. But moving was costly, and Clay was extremely short on cash. Lester jumped at the opportunity to hire the man, promising higher wages and enough money within a year to make his move easily.

Clay Best had lived up to his promise, He cleaned out several rustler gangs and fought the Indians. The ranch began to flourish, and Lester felt confident he was on his way to becoming a very wealthy rancher. Then, while Clay was out of town chasing some renegade Apache, June died without warning. Lester poured another drink and took a sip. *Damned bitch couldn't wait and die once they had moved to Arizona. She had to die right here in Cool Water and ruin everything.*

He had never seen a man go to pieces like Clay Best. When he returned to discover that June had not only passed away, but had been buried in the cemetery, Clay came apart at the seams. He first threatened Lester with the big pistol he carried, then promptly broke every chair in the saloon. Lester had tried to explain that she had died three days before he returned, and that bodies do not keep well in the Texas summer heat, but he refused to be consoled. He left two days later.

Then, things quickly went to hell. As Clay Best was no longer in charge of keeping law and order, the marauders returned in force. His cattle began disappearing in great numbers, so he hired two gunmen, Curley and James Westfall, to stop the thieving. Then, in the middle of everything falling apart, someone kidnapped his granddaughter, Ruth, and held her for ransom.

In desperation, he sent for Clay Best at Carrizo Springs and hired him to find Ruth, only to discover she had actually left on her own, and did not want to return. Then, to add insult to injury, the two men he had hired to stop the thieving were the biggest thieves of all. Curley and James Westfall robbed the bank, killing the teller, and left town with every cent he had. It was later discovered that they had written the note demanding a ransom for Ruth, hoping to bleed him even more.

With no money or cattle, the happy cowboys and dancing saloon girls soon left. The store and bank closed. So did the saloon, with the bartender taking most of the stock in lieu of back wages.

Lester heard the sound of pounding hooves as he poured another drink. "If that's Clay Best, or James Westfall, I'll kill the bastards," Lester said, pulling his Confederate .44 and laying it on the table.

His eyes teared against the dust blowing through the opened window, allowing him to only see shadows as someone entered the saloon.

"What the hell do you want?" Lester growled. He cocked the hammer on the pistol as two more shadows entered the saloon and crossed the room. It wasn't until they were standing at the table that he realized it wasn't Clay Best or James Westfall. The visitors were Mescalero Apache. Lester jerked the pistol upward only to have one of the Indians grab his wrist and twist it upward as he pulled the trigger. The hammer landed with a dull click. Lester cursed and cocked the gun once more as he struggled against the steel-like grip, and received the same result. The Indian finally jerked the gun from his hand and hit him across the face with the pistol. He cursed and begged for mercy as they drug him from the saloon and tied him to a hitching post.

Lester squinted against the sun as a dozen Apache warriors ran to and fro, taking what little he had. Smoke from the burning general store stung his eyes as they set fire to the other buildings. Several braves came from the saloon carrying boxes filled with whiskey bottles. Lester raised his head as the brave that had hit him with the gun stood before him with his hands on his hips.

"You've done enough. Just untie me and leave," Lester said. "I can't do anything to stop you."

The brave grabbed Lester's thinning gray hair and pulled a knife from his belt. Lester's scream drifted on the hot Texas breeze, then fell silent.

Chapter 44

It was approaching mid-afternoon when Clay called a halt. Teresa trotted Diablo forward with Leo in tow and stopped next to Clay. Julio and Estrella stopped a few feet away and sat silently, staring. It wasn't the river, nor even knowing they would be entering Texas very soon, that held their interest. Billows of black smoke rose heavenward in the distance to be carried away by the wind.

"I think there is trouble, huh, *Señor* Clay?" Julio said after a minute.

"I'll say," Clay agreed. He spit and wiped his mouth against a dusty sleeve.

"Do you think it is Cool Water?" Teresa asked.

"Can't be anything else." Clay pulled the spyglass from his saddle bag and adjusted it. He collapsed it a few seconds later and returned it to the saddle bag.

"Can't see nothing clear. There's too much smoke."

"You think it is the work of Indians?" Teresa asked.

"More'n likely that same bunch who decided to camp near the waterfall. What do you think, Julio?"

"*Sí*, I think they were headed to Texas."

"Do you think *Señor* Bishop is okay?" Teresa asked.

"Well, I don't know that answer. I never liked the old bastard, but I hope he made it out okay. I'd hate to think of anyone having to face a bunch of angry Apaches by themselves."

"What do we do now?" Teresa asked.

"Well, we ain't got much choice in the matter. If we stay here, the Federales are likely to catch up with us, and we're gonna have a hard time explaining that bunch we left lying dead back there, and what we're doing with all that gold. On the other hand, if it is Apaches that set fire to Cool Water, they'll likely be gone by the time we get there. They don't normally burn anything until they're done plundering. I'd say we take our chances and mosey on across the river and see what's left of the town. What do you think, Julio?"

"*Sí*," the vaquero said with a nod as he checked his gun.

"That's a good idea for us all," Clay said. "Make sure your guns are loaded and in working order. We might need them either way."

He pulled the spyglass back out of the bag and turned toward Julio with a grin.

"I hate to ask it, but why don't you ride back a mile or so to see if the Federales are following."

"*Bien*," he said with a nod and galloped away.

"Well, let's head for Texas, ladies. And you'd better hang on, Leo, or I'll leave you for the Mexican soldiers to cart off."

They moved forward at a steady walk. The lay of the ground had a gentle slope toward the river, and the arroyo they were following grew shallow and wide. The smell of smoke grew pungent and Clay's eyes started to smart as the wind shifted directly toward them. He looked at Estrella as the girl sneezed several times.

"Hold on a minute," he said and dismounted. He dug around inside one of his saddlebags and came out with two large bandanas, which he handed to the women.

"Here, tie these around your face like this," Clay said, pulling his dusty bandana up just below his eyes.

"You look very much like a bandito," Teresa said with a giggle.

"Will it help with the smoke?" Estrella asked.

"I don't know how much it will help, but it can't hurt none."

"What about *Señor* Leo? Do you have a bandana for him?" Teresa said.

"Leo's got his own tied around his neck. He can shift for himself."

Clay remounted and nudged Loco in the flanks. They continued at the walking pace for the larger part of an hour. Clay was beginning to worry about Julio when he heard the beat of a galloping horse behind. He shifted in the saddle with one hand on the butt of his .44, Then relaxed as Julio exited the arroyo and brought his lathered horse to a halt.

"You had me a little worried, boy. What took so long?"

"I saw a regiment of Federales one mile or more behind. I watched to make sure which way they are heading," Julio said, taking a sip of water from his canteen.

"And? Are they coming?"

"*Sí,*" he said with a nod as he recapped his canteen. "I see one of them studying our tracks, and pointing the way we came. They are following us. That is why I take the arroyo, so maybe they don't see me and give chase."

"That's good thinking. Well ladies," Clay said to the women. "We've been moving at a snail's pace. Are you ready to burn a little leather?"

"*Sí,*" Estrella said, kicking her pony in the flanks.

Clay set the pace at a gentle lope, figuring that was about all the tired animals could keep without collapsing. The smoke grew thicker the closer they came to the river, but it carried with it the scent of water, causing the thirsty animals to increase the pace.

"Better hold 'em in check," Clay yelled as the mules drew beside the horses. "If one of 'em steps in a hole or on a rock, they might bust a leg."

The mule Estrella was leading passed her and would have pulled free of the lead rope, but Julio threw a second rope around his neck and tied it to his large roan. Clay glanced over his shoulder and cursed as the Fererales became visible in the distance.

"Better step it up! They're gaining fast," he yelled.

They were nearing the river when he heard a warning shot. Looking back over his shoulder, he figured they were no more than a half a mile behind.

"Here," he said, handing the lead rope to the mule he had been leading to Teresa. "Take this and don't stop for nothing.

"What are you doing?" she yelled as he turned Loco back.

"Don't ask questions! Just do as I say," he yelled back. "Cross over into Texas as fast as you can and wait for me."

Antonio barked and leaped into the water as they entered the river. Clay brought Loco to a halt a few feet from the water's edge and drew his rifle from its sheath, then watched as the Federales drew closer.

Chapter 45

Captain Ramos collapsed his spyglass and grinned as the big man turned his black horse back from his four companions and drew his rifle. Now, he was waiting in the shallow water with his rifle resting across his saddle as they approached.

"What is he doing?" Lieutenant Flores asked. "He can't honestly think he's going to fight the entire regiment and win."

"No, Clay is not that stupid, my friend," Captain Ramos said, then called a halt to the soldiers.

"Clay? Do you know who he is?" Lieutenant Flores asked.

"Yes, I know Marshal Clay Best quite well, Lieutenant. I've sat in his house and ate at his table. Come, and I'll introduce you."

Captain Ramos turned and gave an order for the regiment to stay approximately fifty yards behind, and not to make any threatening moves. Then he trotted forward with his right hand raised. As they drew closer, Clay turned Loco and galloped through the shallow water to stop again in the middle of the river, where he waited. Julio led the women and mules to the opposite bank and stood in the water with the animals.

"You are going to let them get away?" Lieutenant Flores' voice carried a hint of disbelief. "They are the ones who killed those men back there, and they might be carrying valuable property belonging to Mexico."

"And what if all that is true, Lieutenant? Who, may I ask, did they kill? Was it not Miguel Villa and possibly Manuel Rosales, two desperados we would have killed if we had the chance? And we don't know that they are carrying the gold General Bernal stole, but what if it is true?" He stopped his horse and pointed toward the opposite bank. "Those are women over there. Are you willing to shoot two women for a little stolen gold ... especially when they were not the ones who robbed the payroll train and took the gold?"

Lieutenant Flores stared at him blankly before slowly shaking his head.

"I didn't think so. Besides, I don't think you would want to start your command by crossing the river and causing an international incident between Mexico and The United States, would you?"

"No, *el capitán*, I don't believe I would."

"Good," he said, patting the Lieutenant on the shoulder. "Come, let us go meet with Marshal Best."

They trotted to the center of the river and stopped.

"Ah, Marshal Clay Best, we meet again. It is good to see you, my friend."

"The feeling is mutual, Captain Ramos, but I'm not the marshal anymore," Clay said, shaking the man's hand.

"No? What has happened? Don't tell me they replaced you with someone younger."

"Not exactly. My wife died, so I up and quit. Besides, last time I was in Cool Water, the town had all but died. I didn't figure they needed my services no how."

"I am sorry to hear about your loss. I only met your June one time, but found her to be a great lady," Captain Ramos said. He shifted in his saddle and motioned toward the smoke drifting overhead.

"It would seem that your Cool Water may be under siege."

"Yeah," Clay agreed, shifting to view the sky. "I reckon it might be a band of Mescalero Apaches Julio and me spied a ways back. We figured they might be heading for the border to do some raiding."

"I would be willing to bring my troops across the river and help rid both our countries of this problem, but I'm afraid our two governments would take a dim view if I did."

"And I'm afraid you are right, Captain. I was stretching it a few times when I chased rustlers across the river. But no one except you and me knew anything about it."

"Yes," Captain Ramos said with a chuckle. "It would be much simpler if the politicians would allow us to do our jobs the way we know it should be done, wouldn't it?"

Captain Ramos glanced at Lieutenant Flores and chuckled.

"I am afraid I have been rude toward my officer, *Señor* Best. He is most anxious to meet you. May I present Lieutenant Raoul Flores. He will be taking my command very shortly, as I will be retiring when we get back to the presidio."

"Pleased to meet you, Lieutenant," Clay said with a nod. "I didn't figure you'd ever be anything but a soldier, Captain. What are you going to do with yourself?"

"Juanita and I will be living on the family farm near Juarez and enjoying our grandchildren. You are welcome to come and visit, anytime you wish."

"Might do that sometime."

"Now, perhaps you can answer a question Lieutenant Flores has been dying to ask," Captain Ramos said. "Did you have something to do with those seven dead men lying several hours back on the trail?"

"If you're referring to Miguel Villa and that bunch of highbinders he hung out with, yeah, I reckon we did," Clay said with a nod. "It should've been eight dead. I put two .45 slugs in Manuel Rosales' chest, but he somehow got away. They'd been following us since we left Piedras Negras, then tried to jump us. Rosales held a gun to Teresa's head; said he was gonna kill her if we didn't give him everything we had. I forgot to mention that Teresa and me got married awhile back."

Clay gestured toward Teresa who removed her sombrero and nodded toward them.

"Congratulations," Captain Ramos said. "She's quite lovely."

"Thanks. Anyway, I took exception to him pointing a pistol at my wife's head, and figured a man like Rosales was gonna kill us no matter what we did. So we killed them. Do you blame me?"

"No, but the law might frown on you crossing the border with something that belongs to Mexico, especially gold. May I ask what is packed on those mules?"

"You can ask," Clay said, then took his time packing tobacco into his pipe.

"Well, what is on the mules?" Lieutenant Flores snapped.

"I said he could ask. I didn't say I was gonna answer."

Clay struck a match and lit his pipe as he eyed the Lieutenant.

"Well, I reckon I'd better be moseying toward Cool Water," he said after taking a couple of puffs. "We got a wounded man, and the women will be wanting to change his bandages."

"Since all five of you have crossed the border, there is little I can do to stop you and search the mules. But I feel I must caution you not to cross the border again with something that belongs to Mexico," Captain Ramos said.

"Sounds like good advice. Especially since you're retiring." Clay nodded. "I don't figure the next person would be as understanding as you."

"Now, I will let you go, my friend. Just remember what I said."

"I will," Clay said, shaking the Captain's hand. "Nice meeting you, Lieutenant."

Captain Ramos turned his horse and trotted back toward the waiting regiment as Clay galloped toward Teresa. Lieutenant Flores waited a short minute before following.

"So, that is it? We are letting them go?" Lieutenant Flores asked.

"Yes we are, unless you have a better idea. Don't forget, crossing into the United States to arrest someone without written permission from the United States government is in itself against the law. Besides," he chuckled, "I'm not so sure we would want to start a battle with Clay Best and Julio Garcia."

"Julio Garcia?"

"*Sí*, the young man with him is Julio Garcia, and while I'm not sure, the other could be Leo Santiago. Remember," Captain Ramos grinned at the lieutenant, "there were seven men lying back there, and another that was severely wounded, while only one of the four with *Señor* Best is wounded. We would certainly win the battle, but it would be a costly one. The reason I am allowing this to happen this way is so you will learn an important lesson that will prevent you from making costly mistakes later when you are in charge."

"And what might that be, Captain?"

"The lesson of politics. Much of what you will be dealing with is politics, Lieutenant. Another time, under different circumstances, I might have arrested Clay Best and recovered whatever those mules are carrying. But as for today, what they have will not make any difference to Mexico's future. What will make a difference is for you to have an important ally on the American side of the border. There will be times when it is vital for you to cross into the United States to fight hostile Indians or capture a bandito. Clay Best in an honorable man, and he will aid you with those matters. You will be able to count on his help."

He grinned and swatted the lieutenant on the shoulder.

"Now, order the men to make camp. We will return to the presidio in the morning."

Chapter 46

Sheriff Ray King stamped the dust from his boots and entered the house. His stomach growled as the aroma of spicy pork and fresh tortillas assaulted his nose. His twin boys darted out of the kitchen to wrap their arms around his legs as he hung his hat on the rack and unbuckled his gun belt.

"Hold on there, partners," he said with a grin. "Let me hang my shooting iron first."

He hung the gun belt next to the hat and scooped one boy up in each arm before entering the kitchen.

"How's the prettiest wife in the world?" He leaned to kiss Maria on the lips.

"She is just fine, but Teresa and Clay might take exception to you saying that." Maria tossed the last tortilla on a platter and placed it in the center of the table. "Wash your hands before sitting down."

Ray placed the boys in their highchairs and looked at his hands.

"You really think they need it?"

"Yes, and you should do it every time, if you are going to set an example for the boys."

Ray laughed as he grabbed a bar of lye soap from the wash pan on the sink board.

"I'd planned on washing them in the first place. I had to lock Zeke up again this morning, and he wasn't the cleanest I'd ever seen."

"Again?" Maria said, placing her hands on her hips. "His poor wife. Where does he get the money to buy his whiskey?"

"No telling," Ray said, scooting his chair up to the table. "Now, let's hold hands and thank God for the food," he said to the boys.

He had just finished asking the blessing and was reaching for the platter of tortillas when they heard the first gunshot. Ray took one tortilla off the top and folded it several times as he scooted from the table.

"Say goodbye to your father, he has to go to work," Maria said with a sigh.

Ray stuffed the tortilla in his mouth as several more gunshots sounded. He grabbed his hat and gun belt as a loud pounding sounded on the door.

"Hold your horses, I'm coming," Ray shouted, as more shots mingled with familiar whoops and war cries. His door flung open and Roy Johnson poked his head inside.

"Apaches," Roy said and disappeared.

Ray glanced toward his family, but Maria already had both boys in her arms and was heading toward the basement.

"I have the shotgun. Go!" she yelled as the door to the basement closed. He listened as the heavy bar dropped into place.

Ray pulled the carriage gun from the gun rack above the door and stepped outside. A warrior on horseback charged onto the wooden walkway and was right on top of him as he closed the door. Ray whipped his .45 and fired. The bullet hit the brave in the chest, knocking him from the horse.

He crouched beside the corner of the house, trying to make sense of the chaos that was veiled in a cloud of dust. Roy Johnson appeared from behind a wagon, dressed in his blacksmith's apron, and blew another brave from his horse with a shotgun. One particularly brave warrior leaped from his galloping pony and charged Ray with a lance. One barrel from the twelve-gauge carriage gun sent him pitching backward.

The battle ended almost as fast as it had started. Ray stepped onto the street. He peered up and down the road, waiting for the dust to settle. Roy Johnson silently joined him.

"Well, if that ain't a hell of a note," Roy said after a long minute.

"I reckon," Ray agreed.

"I guess you can tell Maria to finish feeding the boys. I'll take a quick check and let you know what I find," Roy said with a chuckle. "I've been in a couple of tussles with Apaches before, but I've never seen one end this quick."

"Maybe this is why," Ray said, scooping a half-empty whiskey bottle from beside a dead brave. "Could be they were too drunk to give a good fight."

"I think you're right, 'cause they all had a bottle," Charlie Roberts said as he joined them. Charlie was still dressed in his bartending apron, and carrying the shotgun he normally kept under the bar. "One brave had two extra bottles tied around his neck."

He held one of the whiskey bottles up and pointed toward the large C/W on the label.

"I used to tend bar at Lester's saloon in Cool Water, and that's the rot-gut he sold those poor cowboys. I'd bet a platter of Aunt Hattie's sugar cookies they've been to Cool Water before hitting Carrizo Springs."

"Hell," Ray said, tossing the bottle back on the street. "I wonder if anyone was still there."

"Not unless it was ol' Lester. He's all I saw the day I left, not counting Clay and Teresa, and you know they weren't there," Charlie said.

"No, I don't think so, but you'd never know about them two. I thought they'd been back a week ago. No telling where they might be," Ray said, kicking the bottle. "Think you two could take a count and see what damage they might've caused? I'd better give Maria the family signal, or she's liable to shoot the wrong person."

"No problem," Roy said, "but it'll cost you one of Maria's tortillas stuffed with pork."

"How'd you know what we were having?"

"I smelled it when I opened the door."

"Okay, I'll have one for each of you," Ray said as he opened his front door.

******

The final count was twelve dead Apache warriors, two broken windows and three dead horses. Also, Sara Hastings needed stitches to close a cut in her right arm caused by flying glass.

"Shouldn't one of you ride to Cool Water and see if *Señor* Bishop is alright?" Maria asked as she placed more tortillas on the table.

"I reckon, but it's a little late to do it today," Ray said over a mug of coffee. "That's a ten-mile ride. I'll try to get out there early tomorrow."

"Well, if Les was there, we can all guess what happened to him. Arriving tomorrow or in the next day or two won't make a hill's bit of difference," Charlie said.

"He could be alright," Maria said, scrunching her eyebrows. "He might have hid in the basement until they left. You just don't know."

"No, I don't," Charlie said with a nod. "But since all I saw him do the last few weeks I was there was sit inside the saloon and drink his rot-gut whiskey, and since the saloon didn't have a basement, I figure them Apaches found him."

"I only met the man once, and found him to be a honest-to-god jackass, but I'd hate to think what might've happened if he was there," Roy said.

"Well, there's always the chance he was already dead by the time any war party got there," Charlie said.

"What makes you say that?" Ray asked.

"I've seen what that rotgut he wanted me to serve can do. Ol' Dusty was blind as a bat for a whole day after getting drunk on it once. I always figured we were lucky one of the Cool Water punchers didn't die from drinking it."

"Well, I'll try to get out there tomorrow and see what happened. Perhaps one of you boys would care to join me."

"Not me," Charlie said, shaking his head. "I swore I'd never go back the day I left, and I'm keeping that promise."

"I'll go," Roy said. "You do know that several of them were carrying torches. I figure we were lucky they didn't set fire to the livery. But if there wasn't anyone to stop them, they might've burnt Cool Water to the ground. There might not be any Cool Water for us to check on."

"By the way," Charlie said as he reached for another tortilla, "Sara Hastings was asking where we were gonna bury those Indians."

"Why?" Ray asked as he coaxed a spoonful of meat into one of the twins' mouths. "Does she want us to give them a Christian burial?"

"No, just the opposite. She told me she doesn't want them planted anywhere near her late husband. And if we did, she was gonna fill our backsides with buckshot."

"You can tell her she can clean and put that shotgun away. We'll bury them outside the cemetery next to the last bunch of Indians that raided Carrizo Springs."

Chapter 47

Clay sat on horseback viewing the burned out town in front of them. The main house that had belonged to Lester Bishop was a pile of charred and smoking timbers, as well as nearly every cottage or business lining the main road. The bank was destroyed, along with the general store. Empty whiskey bottles were scattered everywhere, which, Clay surmised, was more than likely the reason the saloon was left standing. He figured the Apaches were planning to stop on their return to Mexico. The house that he had shared with June was still standing. A burnt out torch was laying on the porch. It had scorched the dust covered planks, but had failed to ignite. The livery was still intact, due to its construction of adobe walls and earth-covered roof.

Antonio bounded down the road barking, then stopped to hike his leg on a broken down buckboard standing near the saloon. He reached for his pistol as the dog suddenly bristled, and growled at the wagon.

"Wait here 'til I have a look-see," he said to Teresa, and nudged Loco closer to peer into the bed of the wagon, then dismounted. He eased around the buckboard then stopped.

"Aw, hell, Lester!" Clay said, holstering his gun. "You couldn't even die descent, could you?"

Teresa dismounted and led the horse that Leo was riding toward the buckboard. She caught her breath at the sight of Les Bishop's mutilated body tied to the hitching rail behind the wagon.

"*Santa Maria, Madre de Dios.*" Leo Santiago crossed his breast. Teresa and Estrella joined Julio as he repeated the prayer.

"Julio, maybe you and Estrella can check around and see if you can find anyone else," Clay said as he cut the ropes that held Lester to the hitching rail. "Leo, you'd best climb off the cayuse and get out of the sun. I'd hate to bury you next to ol' Les, here."

Clay entered the saloon and lit a lamp as he fished around inside the back store room. He found two dusty blankets, and was leaving the room when he stopped. On a hunch, he rapped against some boards on the back wall with his knuckles. Finding a loose board, he pulled his knife from its sheath and pried it off. He held the lamp high as he felt inside the dark hole.

"Ha!" he said with a grin. Tucked inside the hole were several bottles of expensive brandy. He blew the dust from one of the bottles, then pulled the cork and took a swallow.

"Damn, that was good," he said, recorking the bottle.

Clay tossed the blankets on the ground next to Lester and handed the bottle to Teresa.

"Take a swallow of this and pass it around to the rest."

"Where did you find this?" Teresa ask as she removed the cork.

"I saw Lester hiding several bottles of this back when I first came to Cool Water with June. I didn't figure he ever told anyone where he had it stashed, and I got to thinking the old drunk might've forgotten about hiding it himself. So I checked and sure enough, there it was."

Teresa took a sip and passed the bottle to Leo, then wiped her lips with the back of her gloved hand.

"That is good brandy."

"You bet it is." Clay glared down at Lester for a minute with his hands on his hips.

"Well, I reckon I ought to do something with his body. It's for sure he ain't gonna get no better looking, no matter how long we wait."

"I will have Julio help you dig a grave," Teresa said, then wiped a tear from the corner of her eye.

"Dig a grave?" Clay said indignantly. "I ain't diggin' no grave for the old skinflint. If he wants a grave, let him dig it himself."

"*Santa Maria, Madre de Dios*, please forgive my husband for saying such a thing," Teresa said.

"There ain't nothing to forgive," Clay growled. "The old drunken bastard did nothing but hurt folks and make them miserable his entire life, including his own granddaughter. He ain't worth digging a grave for. I'll wrap his hide in them blankets and drag him off to that wash over yonder. Let the coyotes have him for supper."

Julio and Estrella had returned and were leaning against the saloon wall next to where Leo sat, watching the heated discussion.

"No! You will dig a grave for *Señor* Bishop!" Teresa said, stamping her boot against the wooden walkway.

"I will?" Clay's voice rose as he came closer. "Are you giving me an order?"

"Take it as you wish, *Señor* Best." Teresa gritted her teeth and set her lips into a thin line. "I will give this man a Christian burial if I have to dig the grave myself."

She turned on her heel and walked briskly toward one of the mules and untied a shovel. Clay watched as she marched, shovel in hand, toward the graveyard.

"By damned, I think she means it," he said.

"*Sí*, I think she does," Leo said with a laugh. "I think you should go help her. I will help Julio wrap his body in the blankets."

"Na, you take it easy," Clay said. "Julio can help me dig the grave. Teresa and Estrella can wrap him. I don't want you to open that wound and start bleeding again. Those women have spoiled you enough as it is."

Clay walked briskly to the cemetery and grabbed the shovel from Teresa. "Here, let me do that."

"No, I can do it." She pulled away, but Clay caught the shovel and hung on tight.

"I said I can do it. Just give me a chance."

Teresa released her hold on the shovel and stepped back with her hands on her hips.

"Thank you," Clay said with a hint of sarcasm. He turned and walked between graves to the far corner of the small cemetery. Teresa watched as he sank the shovel into the rocky soil and tossed the dirt aside.

"I started to dig the grave here," she said, pointing toward the tiny hole at her feet.

"Yeah, I know. And you were doing a fine job of it." He tossed more dirt aside. "But that's mighty close to June's grave, and I ain't burying that rotten bastard anywhere near June, or Billy Mayfield." He sank the shovel and took another bite from the earth as Julio joined him.

"I ain't quite got shed of the feeling that me bringing June here, and they way Les treated us, had something to do with her dying. And, I know for a fact that he cheated Billy out of five thousand dollars, then laughed when Billy got hisself killed." He pitched another shovelful of dirt aside.

"Now, why don't you go help that girl wrap that polecat in those blankets, while Julio and me dig this grave?"

"*Bien.*" Teresa wiped her eyes with her knuckles and joined Estrella at the buckboard.

"That woman's gonna drive me to drink," Clay grumbled as he removed his jacket and rolled his shirt sleeves.

"That's okay," Julio said with a snicker. "I have more tequila in my saddlebag."

"That's good. We'll drink it with supper, then wash it all down with that bottle of ten-year-old brandy. I know where Lester kept his stash, and there's still several bottles, if we need it."

"Ah, then maybe we will salute him when we drink it, eh?" Julio said with a grin.

"Yeah, maybe we will at that."

******

Clay tossed the last of the dirt on the grave and packed it down with several whacks of the shovel. Julio finished tying two half-straight mesquite branches together in the shape of a cross and drove it into the head of the grave. The men removed their hats as Teresa and Estrella draped scarves of black Spanish lace over their heads and knelt in prayer. Clay leaned against the fence, thinking Teresa was taking her sweet time trying to pray Les' soul into heaven. He figured where Les was, all the prayers in the world wouldn't be doing him much good now.

She finished by crossing her breast in the name of the Father, Son and Holy Ghost, then kissing her crucifix.

"Well?" she said, looking at Clay. "That little prayer didn't kill you, now did it?"

"No, I don't reckon it did at that." Clay draped his jacket over his shoulder and lit his pipe. "Les always claimed to be a Presbyterian, not a Catholic. But most Presbyterians I know are Bible-believing, hell-fearing folks, and I never knew Les to look at a Bible, much less believe in what it says. I sure hope he drank his fill while he was alive, 'cause he sure ain't going to be drinking nothing now."

Teresa stopped halfway to Clay's old house and crinkled her brow at him.

"Why are you being so, so hateful? Why can't you forgive him, now that he's dead?

"Well, that's fine talk coming from you. The last time we came here, you were the one cussin' him to his face, and you pulled that pearl-handled pistol. I had to grab your arm to keep you from blowing him into hell back then."

"That was because he lied and was cheating us out of a thousand dollars," she snapped.

"Yeah, he did lie and cheat us," Clay said with a nod. "But he still owes us the thousand dollars, and I don't think he's gonna be giving it to us, do you? So, you tell me. What makes the difference?"

Teresa burst into tears and ran inside the house, slamming the door.

"What'd I do wrong?" Clay asked as Estrella glared at him. "All I did was ask a simple question."

Estrella disappeared silently into the house, as Leo and Julio laughed.

"You will never understand her, *Señor* Clay. She is a woman," Leo said.

"Yeah, so she is," Clay said. "So was June. A real lady. But June was sort of like me. She liked things simple, and easy to understand." Clay motioned with his hand like he was smoothing a tablecloth. "But Teresa is getting worser. Her moods bounce all over the place."

"Mmm, maybe she's not feeling well. She vomited the past two mornings. Maybe she's sick and should see a doctor," Leo said.

"Yeah, that's what Julio's been saying, and I figure it's not a bad idea," Clay said with a nod. "I'll have the doctor take a look at her when he looks at you."

"Julio, where's that bottle of brandy?"

"I think it's inside the *casa* with the women. But I still have the tequila," Julio said.

"Well, fetch it. Then, after we've had a snootful, we'll see to the animals."

******

Teresa and Estrella fixed a sparse dinner of tortillas, canned beans, jerked beef, and hot coffee. Clay retrieved the bottle of Les' brandy and they sat on the porch, enjoying the cool evening breeze. Julio had noticed black clouds rolling in over the Anacacho Mountains late in the afternoon, and now commented on the dark sky. One of the mules in the corral stamped his feet and hee-hawed loudly, as the low rumble of thunder sounded in the distance.

"It's amazing how they hear the thunder before we do," Leo said as Teresa added more brandy to his tin cup.

"Yeah, just so's it's the thunder they're hearing," Clay said. "We'd better stay alert tonight. If those mules start kicking up a fuss, it might be the Apaches returning for another drink.

"Look!" Estrella said, pointing as lighting danced in the black sky. It was followed by more rolling thunder.

"How far away?" Teresa asked.

"Mmm, hard to tell. Fifteen, maybe twenty miles," Clay said. "What do you think, Julio?"

"*Sí*, maybe closer," he said with a nod.

They finished the pot of coffee and had nearly emptied the bottle of brandy when the wind suddenly picked up. It felt cool, and brought with it the distinct smell of rain.

"I think we are going to get wet," Leo said as several large raindrops splatted against the porch.

"Could be, but it just might be teasing us," Clay said. He had no more than gotten the words out of his mouth when the sky suddenly opened up.

"Holy cow!" Clay yelled as the wind whipped large drops of rain at them. The women squealed and dashed inside the house.

"Come on, grab your grip and move inside," he yelled once more.

They crowded at the windows and watched as the torrent continued.

"It is going to be crowded in here," Teresa said, pointing toward the saddles and gear they had moved from the porch.

"Well, maybe we can figure out something," Clay said. "If it let's up, we might be able to stash them inside the saloon. Although I'd hate to leave all that gold unguarded over night."

"We could store the gold in the corner," Julio said, "and take the saddles to the cantina."

"Sounds good." Clay nodded thoughtfully. "Of course, we might be able to stick the saddles back on the porch, if it quits blowing."

The wind whipped the rain against the front of the house for the space of a half an hour. Clay had almost decided that he and Julio were going to have to brave the storm and carry the saddles to the saloon, when the wind died to a gentle breeze. He opened the door and watched the downpour, then waited a few more minutes before stepping out onto the porch.

"Well, it washed all the dirt away," he said with a chuckle. "Might as well bring the saddles out and cover them with a tarp. I think it will be safe enough."

Julio helped stack the saddles and bridles into a neat pile and cover them, while Teresa and Estrella put their blankets on the bed and made pallets on the floor for the men. Clay lit his pipe and leaned against one of the posts, watching the rain. Estrella came from the house and stood on the lower step and leaned over to wash her long hair in the rain.

"Actually, that ain't a bad idea," Clay said. He laid the pipe aside and removed his gun belt and hat, then stood in the rain with his face turned upward. It wasn't but a matter of seconds before everyone but Leo was getting soaked. Teresa finished by leaving one of the wash pans on the steps to be filled with fresh rain water.

"Hot damn, I'd forgotten what good Texas rainwater feels like," Clay said as he relit the pipe. "I think we're all going to sleep a little better tonight."

******

Clay woke at daybreak feeling good about life in general. He had moved his sleeping arrangement to the front porch, and was joined by both Julio and Leo, who complained that the house was too warm and cramped inside.

"Can't argue with you on either count, since I felt the same while living here," he said.

Clay stretched, then stared as Antonio came trotting in with a rabbit in his mouth.

"If you're gonna have breakfast, eat that thing over yonder on the other end of the porch. I don't wanna have to watch you this morning."

The women were still sleeping when he slipped inside and stoked the stove. He had the coffee on when Teresa yawned and stretched her lean body in bed.

"*Buenos días, marido*. How are you this morning?"

"Your husband is just fine. The question is, how are you feeling today? You were acting out of sorts yesterday, and I think you might've had a touch of something."

"*Bien*, I feel good." Teresa smiled, then looked toward the girl lying beside her as Estrella stirred and opened her eyes.

"That's good," Clay said with a nod. "Now, I'll leave you two alone while you dress. Me and Julio will check on the animals and pack the gear. You can fix whatever you want to eat. Coffee's fine for me."

He closed the door and nudged Julio with the toe of his boot.

"Get up, you lazy varmint. It's time to pack and head home." Clay lit his pipe and hummed a tune as he headed toward the corral.

"Dang, some clean clothes, a hot bath and a shave are shore going to feel good."

Chapter 48

Ray King stood on the porch sipping a mug of coffee as he watched Roy Johnson and Charlie Roberts. The men were caked with mud, and struggling to help Harley Sorenson pull his heavy hay wagon from a mud hole in front of the blacksmith shop. At the present, Harley was cursing and beating his mules to no effect. He stopped when Ruth Collier, the parson's wife, came from her house and yelled for him to quit using profanity while the town's children were present.

Ray craned his neck for a better view of the street. "Huh," he said to himself. The woman was right. There were several small knots of children pointing toward the men and laughing.

He drained the coffee and set the empty mug down, then waded through the mud toward the wagon.

"Roy, why don't you grab a couple more mules from the livery and hitch 'em up? You might have more success."

"I thought about it, but this idgit picked the biggest puddle he could find to drive his wagon through. Now, it's buried up to the axle. I don't think two, or even four extra mules is gonna help."

"This is the way I always come when I'm delivering hay. I pull through here and swing the mules thata way," Harley pointed toward Ray's house. "That way, I can back the wagon right inside, next to the lean-to where you store the hay."

"Yeah, but that's the first rain we've had in more'n a coon's age," Charlie growled. "It wouldn't have hurt you none to use a little common sense and shy away from this lake."

"Well, then I'd suggest you quit beating those poor animals and unload the wagon," Ray said with a shrug.

"Unload it here?" Harley asked.

"That's what I said."

"What are we going to do with the hay? We can't stack all this hay in the mud. It'd ruin it."

"Good Lord, Harley," Ray said with a laugh. "Stack the hay in the lean-to where Roy stores his hay, just like you always do."

"How in the hell do you expect me to do that? The lean-to is all the way over there, Ray. I've got a wagon-load of hay here. What do you expect me to do, carry it on my back?" Harley grew red in the face as he yelled.

"No, I've never carried hay on my back, but I have used pitchforks to move it into another wagon or wheelbarrow. I've also carried a few armloads and dumped it where I wanted it to go. Now, I'd suggest you get busy unloading the rig, unless you've got a better idea."

Ray turned his back and laughed as Harley began cursing a blue streak. He waded carefully, picking the least muddy trail back toward the porch. Maria came from the house, carrying the coffee pot, and refilled his cup.

"You don't need to tell him, but I sometimes think that Harley Sorenson is not very smart," she said with a giggle.

"Well, I think you've got that right. He's not stupid, by any means, but he doesn't stop to think some things through. No one in their right mind would drive a loaded hay wagon through the biggest mud hole they could find."

"Are you going to go to Cool Water this morning?"

"I was thinking about it, but the road looks pretty nasty. I think I'll wait until tomorrow. One day ain't gonna make much difference, if those Apaches were there."

They paused to watch the scene in the middle of the road as Harley started it up again.

"That's it," Roy said, and threw the hay he had back into the wagon. "You can unload the wagon by your own self, you ornery bastard."

"I'll be damned if I'm going to unload this wagon by myself," Harley yelled. "If you want this hay, you'll pitch in and help unload."

"That's what I was doing, you numb-skull. But I ain't used to being cussed at by someone that I'm offering a helping hand to, especially when I'm buying it and paying you to deliver it."

"You'll damn sure help unload, if you want another delivery!" Harley yelled.

"Are you threatening me?"

Ray set the mug of coffee down and headed back toward the wagon as Roy came toward Harley carrying a pitchfork.

"Whoa, whoa, you two. Hold on there, Roy," Ray said. "Let's just settle down before this gets serious."

"It's already serious," Roy yelled. "If he calls me one more name, I'm going to rip his guts out." Roy shook the pitchfork in the air.

"And I'll by damned blow yer head off." Harley reached under the wagon seat for his shotgun.

"All right, that's enough!" Ray yelled. "Here, give me that." He snatched the pitchfork from Roy's hand. "And you," he pointed toward Harley, "either you hand over that scatter-gun, or I'm going to lock you up until Jesus comes in his glory." He snapped his fingers and held out his hand.

"I'm serious, Harley. Give me the gun ... now!"

Harley glared at Roy as he slowly passed the shotgun to Ray.

"Now, up on my porch. Both of you." Ray stepped back and pointed toward his house, where Maria was holding one of the twins and grinning at the men.

"I'm not kidding. I want the both of you up there now, or I'm going to lock you in one of those cells."

"On what charge?" Harley asked with a sneer.

"Which one do you want? Disturbing the peace? Using profanity in the presence of women and children? Threating a citizen with a loaded fire arm? Want me to keep going? The list is pretty long, and it could get costly if you want to keep acting like a jackass." Ray grabbed his arm and glared at Roy.

"You too, up on the porch. We're going to settle this right here and now."

Ray made them sit in chairs on opposite sides of the porch. Once he thought he had them calm enough, he grinned at his wife.

"Maria, why don't you let me hold Matt, while you bring these two a cup of coffee?"

"*Bueno*," she said with a laugh and handed him the wiggly boy. "But I think they need more than coffee."

"That's not a bad idea," Ray said with a nod. "Pour a generous portion of Tennessee sour mash in each cup. Maybe it'll change their disposition."

He waited until they each had their cups and had taken a couple of sips. He took a sip from his own cup and grinned, realizing Maria had not forgotten about him.

"Okay, I know you're both flustered, but there's no reason to take this where you guys were heading. You've been friends too long for something like that."

"That's what I thought," Roy said. "But I'm not gonna stand for anyone calling me names like that."

"And I don't think you should. But you can't threaten to rip someone's insides out with a pitchfork and not expect them to reach for something to defend themselves with.

"As for you," Ray said, glaring at Harley. "Don't ever point a shotgun at someone in Carrizo Springs again. If you do, you'd better have a damned good reason."

"I thought that pitchfork was reason enough," Harley said.

"In most cases, that might be true. But not this one. Neither of you had any call to be carrying on the way you were."

Ray took a sip of coffee and exhaled deeply.

"Now, here's what's going to happen. The both of you are gonna head over to the schoolhouse and hire several strappin' boys to come help stack this hay."

"Hire them?" Harley yelled.

"That's what I said. Hire them. And you're gonna give them fair wages for doing the work."

"That'll mean I'm paying a second time for hay that I've already paid for," Roy growled.

"You got a better plan?" Ray asked.

"Hell, I can't afford to do that, Ray. That'll mean I'll be selling all this hay for nothing. What's in it for me? I've gotta live too."

"You want to unload all that hay by yourself?" Ray glared at Harley. "I didn't think so," he added as Harley lowered his eyes toward his muddy boots.

"The fact is, neither of you are gonna empty that load by arguing and threatening to kill one another. All that's going to do is cause one of you to do something stupid, and I'll have to lock you up. And..." Ray pointed a finger at Harley, you're not going to move that wagon until it's empty, and that's a fact. It's buried up to its axles, and beatin' and cussing your mules isn't gonna do nothing but frustrate some good animals."

Ray leaned back in his chair and grinned.

"Now, both of you finish your coffee and go find some help to unload that hay."

Chapter 49

The women prepared a light breakfast of tortillas, warm jerked beef and coffee. They ate on the front porch, and chattered happily about the adventure that was almost over, and what they were going to do once they reached Carrizo Springs.

"Once I am well enough, I am going to return to Piedras Negras and see my wife and son," Leo said, leaning back against the front wall.

"Well, when that day comes, we won't send you away empty-handed," Clay said quietly. Teresa smiled at him.

"*Gracias, Jefe*," Leo said with a slow nod.

"How about you, Julio?" Clay asked.

"Estrella and I are going to visit my father. He has a small rancho near Nuevo Laredo, and we will get married there."

"Oh," Clay arched his eyebrows and nodded. "I knew you two were kind of joined at the hip, but I didn't know it was that serious. Congratulations. I hope to see you again sometime."

"*Gracias*, we will not stay. My older brother runs the rancho, and we do not agree on many things. But my father is an old man, and I would like him to meet Estrella before he dies."

"That's understandable. You'll have more than enough money for a good start." Clay sipped his coffee and grinned as Teresa hugged the girl.

******

They hadn't ridden more than a mile before Teresa dismounted and ran to vomit behind a tree.

"That does it," Clay barked as she climbed back into the saddle. "You're seeing Doc Phillips first thing when we hit town, and no arguing."

Teresa studied him for a few seconds before grinning. "Don't worry so much, *mi amor*. I feel much better now."

"I said, no arguing."

He nudged Loco in the flanks and they started moving once more. A roadrunner darted across the road in front of them and several jack rabbits bounded through the brush. They crossed a wash that had collected several puddles of rain water. A small antelope drinking from one of the puddles looked up at them and darted off. The lowing of cattle caught his attention and he brought Loco to a stop.

"Well, would you take a look at that," he said, pointing toward a longhorn bull guarding his small harem of four cows while they grazed in the brush. "I guess they are some of Lester's that the rustlers missed."

Clay felt good inside. He couldn't have explained why, but he suddenly felt as though he'd come home. He inhaled a deep breath and exhaled slowly.

"Boy, there's nothing like the smell of desert air after a good rain. I've always loved the smell of sage and clean air. You ain't gonna find that in a hole like Piedras Negras, Leo."

"No, I won't," Leo shook his head as he studied Clay.

"Ya know," Clay shifted in the saddle to look at the others. "That old miserable skinflint might've been kin to Satan himself, but he sure picked a good hunk of land to raise cattle on."

"I thought you said this was the closest place to Hades you had seen," Teresa said.

"Yeah, I might've. But that was because we're in the middle of a drought, and I was working for that bag of bones we buried back yonder. Some day, this drought is gonna break, and with Lester gone, Cool Water could be a downright pleasant place to be."

"What are you thinking," Teresa asked with a laugh.

"What I'm thinking is, we're looking to buy a place to raise cattle, ain't we? Why not Cool Water? Once it starts raining, there'll be plenty of grass, and the spring runs year-round."

He nudged Loco and they started moving.

"With ol' Lester gone, I reckon the place belongs to his granddaughter Ruth. I think I'll talk to her, and see if she's willing to sell."

"What if she doesn't want to sell," Leo said.

"Well, then I'll just have to find another place to buy, won't I?"

Clay guided Loco around a clump of cactus.

"I remember you once said that Cool Water was a place for thieves and robbers, and not fit for cattle," Teresa said with a grin. "There's a good chance it will still be that way."

"Maybe it was, but that was because Les Bishop didn't know beans about running a ranch."

"And you do?" She giggled.

"You don't think I do?" Clay scowled at her.

"I didn't say that. All I've known is that you were a lawman. I've never heard you say you were a vaquero."

"Well, for your information, miss smarty-pants, I grew up on a cattle ranch. I was punching cattle by the time I was old enough to walk. What do you think of that?"

"*Bien*, that is good," Teresa said as she laughed. "I just think you're cute when you get excited about something. But we are only two people, my love, and this is a big place. How are we going to build a ranch and raise cattle by ourselves?"

"Well, I reckon we'll just have to hire some men. Unless...now this is just an idea...if we knew some good men who would like to invest in a good hunk of land and go into business with us, you know, be partners. Well, I just might be willing to consider such a proposition." He eyed Julio and Leo. "It's something to think about."

******

They rode into Carrizo Springs midafternoon, and wove their way through the muddy street and around the teen-age boys unloading the hay. The wagon was almost empty, and Clay stopped to lean in the saddle and eye the buried axle. He waved at Ray King, who was supervising the unloading from his front porch.

"I reckon they're still gonna have a time pulling it outa that mud hole," Clay yelled.

"I reckon you might be right." Ray toasted them with his coffee mug and grinned. "Good to see you back."

"Good to be back." Clay nudged Loco forward.

Teresa took Estrella and Leo to the house while Clay and Julio tied the mules in front of the bank. They untied the load on one mule and Clay grabbed two bags. He entered the bank and dropped the heavy load on the counter, then eyed the surprised teller.

"Where do you want this, Johnny? There's more coming."

"Mr. Jenkins," the young man yelled toward the back. Henry Jenkins came from the back office as Julio dropped two more bags on the counter. Clay turned to follow him out.

"What's all this?" Henry asked.

"It's exactly what it looks like, Hank. Gold," Clay said. The banker was staring wide-eyed as the men returned carrying more bags.

"How many bags do you have?" Henry asked as he came around the counter and headed toward the window.

"Two mules worth. Now where do you want it stacked?"

"Good Lord!" Henry's voice sounded shrill. "Bring it back here." He propped the swinging gate open and pointed toward a large table. "Put the bags on the floor. It's going to take some time to count."

Henry ran back to the window and flipped the sign to read *closed.*

It took almost ten minutes to unload both mules and carry the gold inside. A sizeable crowd had gathered in front of the bank by the time the task was complete, and Clay ignored several questions as he carried the last two bags inside the bank.

"I'm gonna mosey on down to the house, Hank, and leave you two to finish counting," Clay said.

"Wait, don't you want to stay and supervise the counting?" Henry asked.

"Na, I figure you ain't gonna cheat me, and we're both beat to the bone. Just split it five ways. One account will be in mine, and another in Teresa's name. One account under Julio Garcia's name, a fourth account for Leo Santiago, and the last one will be for a girl named Estrella. I don't know her last name. Do you Julio?"

Julio shook his head.

"You're fixin' to marry her and you don't know her last name?"

"No," he said with a shrug. "It doesn't seem that important when we're together."

"Just open her an account, Hank. We'll give you her name tomorrow. Come to think of it, I don't know if she knows how to read or write."

"Yes, sir. Anything else?" Henry asked as Clay opened the door.

"No, not that I can think of. Just give me a total in the morning."

Chapter 50

Teresa and Estrella let Leo bathe first, then took their time dressing the wound. They were washing each other's hair in the lean-to attached to the back of the house when Clay and Julio entered the house. Clay stared at Leo, who was snoring loudly on his bed.

"I think it will be hard to sleep here tonight," Julio said.

"Yeah, I agree. I'm thinking of renting a room at the hotel for him," Clay said.

"Maybe I will rent a room also."

"Leave your valuables here if you do," Clay said. "I rented one when I first came to Carrizo Springs, and found that someone rifled though my belongings."

Julio nodded, then looked at Clay and grinned as Teresa's laughter was followed by Estrella giggling.

"Sounds like they're having a passel of fun," Clay said.

"Maybe we should take the mules and horses to Miguel's stable at the edge of town," Julio said.

"Sounds like good advice."

******

"Ah, it is good to see you, *Señor* Best," Miguel said, grasping Clay's hand firmly. "You've been gone a long time. How is Teresa? I hope she is well."

"I reckon she's doing just fine. She's back at the house trying to scrub some of the trail dust off."

"Tell her there is no need for her to cook tonight. My Juanita will be happy she's returned, and will cook dinner. It will give her a chance to find out everything that happened, and tell Teresa all the gossip in town."

"That'll be fine, but I'd better warn you that we've picked up a couple of stragglers along the way. We've got a young Indian girl, and Leo Santiago at the house. He got himself plugged and needs to see the doc."

"It is no problem. I shall bring some wine and tequila. That will give us something to drink while the women talk."

The women were still in the washroom when they returned, and Leo was still snoring.

Clay clasped Julio around the shoulders and guided him back out into the street.

"If he's married, I don't know how in the hell his wife can stand to sleep with him. Come on. We'll scrub down at the bathhouse. Then, we can get fortified before tonight's wingding. Miguel has six children, and a couple of them are anything but calm."

******

Clay quickly finished one mug of beer and ordered two more as Julio polished his mug off.

"So, have you heard about the Apache attack while you were gone?" Charlie asked.

"No, we just got back. When did it happen?"

"Day before yesterday. They came charging down the street whooping and yelling as bold as brass."

"Anyone hurt?" Clay asked.

"Sara Hastings needed a couple of stitches from a cut she got on her arm when one of them savages busted her window. But other that that, no. Just twelve dead Apaches."

Clay looked at Julio. "Think it was them that we saw?" The vaquero shrugged, then nodded.

"Where'd y'all see them?" Charlie said.

"Down in Mexico, on our way back."

They looked up as Ray King joined them at the bar and ordered a beer.

"You look a little worse for wear, but I reckon you'll do," Ray said.

"Charlie was telling me about the Apaches kicking up some trouble," Clay said.

"They tried, but not much happened."

"Clay was saying they'd seen some down in Mexico before they got here," Charlie said.

"That right?"

"Could be the same ones. We saw twelve braves, and hid out in a cave until they left," Clay said.

"Well, you didn't happen to ride through Cool Water on your way back, did you?" Charlie asked as he leaned against the counter. "We found some bottles of Lester's rotgut on them."

"Yeah, we did happen through there yesterday. Not much left of the place. They burned it to the ground, all except the saloon and my old house. They even burnt Lester's mansion. They tried to torch my place, but it didn't take."

"What about Les Bishop?" Ray asked. "Was he still there?"

"Yeah, I reckon he was, or what's left of him. They filled him with arrows and took what little hair he had. We buried him in the cemetery."

"Damn," Charlie shook his head, "I hated his guts, but losing your hair to an Apache? Dammit!"

Charlie drifted down the bar to fill someone's order.

"Hank says you deposited nearly half a million in Mexican gold and silver in his bank," Ray said.

"Really? That much?" Clay arched his eyebrows at Julio.

"That's what he said. I'm not askin' where you got it," Ray said, staring at the mirror behind the bar.

"That's good," Clay said. He took a sip of beer and snickered.

"I didn't rob no bank or hold up a train, if that's what you're worried about."

"That was one of the things," Ray said with a nod. "But it does cause one to wonder where a busted-down lawman like you got his mitts on that much gold and silver. I'm responsible for law and order here, and it does make me curious."

"Hell, Ray. I know a little about the law myself," Clay said.

"I know you do, and I didn't think Clay Best would rob a bank. Besides, I don't think any bank around here would have that much gold."

"If you must know, it was stolen money, but Julio and me didn't steal it. Bernal and his men robbed a Federale payroll train a few years back. Teresa was married to Refugio at the time, and they made off with a wagonload of gold and silver. Bernal couldn't haul that much around, so he had Refugio and a couple of men hide it. After they had it stashed, he decided to stop off here and see Teresa before returning to Bernal. Then the Comanches decided to raid Carrizo Springs at the same time."

"And that's the raid where Refugio and his men got themselves killed right in front of Teresa's place," Ray said with a nod.

"That's about the size of it. Teresa said she waited for Bernal to send someone to find out where the money was hidden, but that never happened. And when he finally got around to sending someone, they asked to see Refugio. She told them Refugio had gotten killed, and showed them the grave, and they left. So...," Clay paused to take a sip of beer, "since she knew where it was hidden, we went to see if it was still there."

Clay turned to eye Ray. "That's only part of what they hid, Ray. There's that much or more still sitting there."

"The hell you say!" Ray took a swig of beer.

"Yes, the hell I say. The trouble is, the place is crawling with Comanches, Apaches and Yaquis, not to mention the Federales. We even ran into some of Bernal's old gang, and had to fill them with lead before crossing the Rio Grande." Clay shook his head and laughed. "It wasn't easy, that's for sure."

"What are you going to do now?" Ray asked.

"I'm going to head home, eat a good dinner, then sleep as long as I can. when I wake up, I'm going to see about buying a hunk of land and raise some cattle."

"Sounds like a good plan," Ray said.

"*Perdóname*," Julio said, leaning to get a good look at Ray. "What happened to the young *chica* we saved?"

"You mean Roberta Sawyer?"

"*Sí.*" Julio nodded.

"Roberta died the next day. She's buried at the church next to her parents."

Julio shook his head and crossed his chest, then cursed in Spanish.

"Speaking of which," Ray said. "I got a telegram from Ranger Hart, telling what happened to the ones that got away. Nice piece of work...all of you."

"Yeah, only they died too quick. I would've made 'em suffer just a little, if I had my druthers," Clay said. He ordered another round of beers.

"I can't blame you," Ray agreed.

"By the way, I've got a couple of mules belonging to the Sawyers. Reckon they've got any relatives that want them?"

"I'll check and see," Ray said. "Well, I'd best get back to work and earn what little this town's paying me."

"Yeah, we'd better head toward the house too, before Teresa skins us alive." Clay downed the last of his beer and wiped his moustache against his sleeve.

Chapter 51

Clay stared out the window while the train slowed as it entered San Antonio. Teresa's head lay against his shoulder and rocked gently with the movement of the car. While she was still trim and beautiful, she was starting to show, and had been asleep for most of the trip. It had been a month of changes for both of them. The first and greatest shock came the day following their arrival in Carrizo Springs, when he stood in Doctor Phillips' waiting room.

"They are both fine, Mr. Best," the doctor said with a grin. "Whatever it was that your wife and that Indian girl were putting on Mr. Santiago's wound certainly kept it from getting infected."

"Hang Leo, Doc. I want to know what's ailing Teresa," Clay snapped.

"Nothing is *ailing* her. Your wife and baby are just fine."

Clay stared at the doctor for a few seconds before screwing up his face.

"Baby? What baby?"

"Your baby. Mrs. Best is approximately three months pregnant. You are going to be a father (God help the child)."

Teresa was adjusting her dress as she came from the examining room beaming at Clay. She rushed into his arms and repeatedly kissed his face.

"We are having a baby!" she squealed.

That was only the beginning. After suffering the ribbing he received from Ray King and Miguel Rios about becoming a daddy, Leo Santiago informed him that he wanted to leave the majority of his money in the bank as payment for a share in Clay's future cattle ranch.

"But I ain't got one yet, Leo. I still need to talk to Ruth Stanley about buying the Cool Water Ranch. They might decide to keep the place, and even if they sell it, it might be several years before it starts paying for itself."

"*Sí, amigo*. But this weather, it will change, no? And with my share of the money, you will be able to buy a much larger rancho and stock it with fine cattle. And when it starts to rain we will own a *muy bueno* rancho."

"Well, I can't find any flaws in your thinking," he said with a nod. "But instead of you tossing all your money into a venture that might turn belly-up, how about me selling you 20%? That way you can hang onto some money to take care of that wife and son you've been talking about?"

"*Bueno, Señor* Clay. *Bueno*," Leo said, pumping Clay's hand.

Leo promptly withdrew a small amount of money and borrowed a wagon from Miguel at the stable. Stocking the wagon with a few supplies, Leo headed toward Piedras Negras to collect his wife and son. He returned two weeks later with a chunky teenage girl and a one-year-old boy. Figuring he should give them something to do, Clay bought a large Studebaker wagon and a team of horses.

"I reckon you'd best start cleaning up the townsite. You can stay at my old place, and haul the burnt rubble to the arroyo south of town. Save anything that looks useable. I should be back in plenty of time before you're finished. Then we can think about adding a couple of new houses before we buy cattle."

******

Julio followed Clay to the bench and sat beside him, sipping his evening coffee. Teresa and Estrella were chatting happily inside the *jacale* as they cleaned the supper dishes.

197

Clay chuckled as Antonio scooted an empty bowl that had once contained table scraps across the yard."Ya know, licking that bowl ain't gonna make more food appear," he said.

Julio cleared his throat as he set the mug aside.

"*Señor* Clay? Estrella and me have been talking."

"That's understandable." Clay grinned.

"Well, I wanted to ask if we could also buy a part of the rancho."

"I reckon you might. Me and Teresa kinda figured on you and the girl being a part. Since you're fixin' to marry that girl, I'll give you and Estrella the same deal I gave Leo. I'll sell you 20% as a couple. That way you can still hang onto some of that money in case this doesn't work out. Sound fair enough to you?"

"*Bueno*," Julio said with a nod. "That is good."

Julio and Estrella left their funds in the bank, much to Henry Jenkins' delight. They withdrew only a small amount and were married by the priest in the church, then left to visit his father at Nuevo Laredo. They returned three weeks later, with news that his father had died. Julio said his brother had things at the rancho under control, so there wasn't any reason for him to stay. Clay sent the young couple to help Leo with the clean up.

Clay had mixed feelings when Ray King informed him that Roberta Sawyer had relatives in Houston, who were giving the mules to him as a way of saying *thank you* for helping to administer justice to her slayers. While they were fine animals, and he was happy to keep them, George Sawyer was a friend, and he felt he owed them something. He again offered to pay for the mules, but they sent him a telegram declining his offer.

******

The train jolted to a stop and Teresa raised her head.

"We have arrived?" she said, rubbing her eyes.

198

"Yes, we're in San Antonio, sleepyhead." He smiled at her. "Now, we've got to collect our bags and check into a hotel."

Clay asked the cabbie to take them to the same hotel they had stayed in on their last visit to San Antonio. He liked the hotel's location adjacent to the depot, and the friendly atmosphere, but he especially liked the food in the restaurant. Since Teresa had not insisted on bringing Antonio on this trip, the hassle of caring for the large dog wasn't an issue.

They both bathed and took a relaxing afternoon nap before dining in the downstairs restaurant.

"What are you going to name your son?" Teresa asked over her cup of coffee.

"I haven't given it much thought. It could be a girl, you know."

"*Sí,*" she said with a nod. "What would you name your daughter?"

"I don't rightly know that either. I reckoned we'd discuss that issue together when the time got closer."

"I think we should name our son Clay, after his father," she said with a grin.

"Well, I don't know about that," Clay said with a snort. "I've never been partial to the name myself. I don't hate it, but there's a few names I like better."

"Like what?"

"I don't know," he said with a snicker. "How about Wyatt or Morgan? The Earp brothers have done alright for themselves."

Teresa leaned across the table and gave him a crooked grin.

"If I'm not mistaken, Morgan got killed, and his brother Virgil got wounded. Am I correct?"

"Yes, you're correct, but Morgan died keeping law and order."

"*Sí,* but I would rather have our son keep law and order and stay alive. I like Clay."

"Well, if it means that much to you, call him Clay. I'll probably call him *son* anyway. How about Teresa if she's a girl?"

"No," Teresa laughed. "I think Elena Maria Rosetta Clay."

"That's quite a handle. How come so many names?"

"Elena is for my mother. Maria is for my grandmother, and Rosetta is for my sister. I should have more for my godmother and my sister's daughter, but that would be too many names, I think."

"Yeah, I think it's a little much too," Clay said with a nod. He took a sip of wine and squeezed her hand.

Teresa covered his hand with hers and smiled. "I was also thinking of naming her June after your first wife."

Clay grew somber for a second before nodding slowly. "I think that's a nice gesture, and she'd like it. But why? You never met her."

"I think I know her well, and I like her."

Clay swirled the wine in his glass thoughtfully. "I think I'm going to let you name our children since you've given this so much thought."

******

Clay rapped on the large oak door three times with the brass knocker and stepped back to hold Teresa's arm inside of his. The door opened seconds later. Yolanda, the Stanley's maid, eyed them briefly before breaking into a broad smile.

"*Señor* Clay, *Señorita* Romero. It is good to see you again. Come in, *por favor*. *Señora* Stanley will be happy to see you."

"It is now *Señora* Best," Teresa said as they entered the large Victorian. "*Señor* Clay and I were married four months ago."

"No!" the maid exclaimed. "*Señora* Stanley will be happy to hear that." She grabbed Teresa's hand and led her toward the parlor, leaving Clay to follow.

"*Señor* and *Señora* Best to see you, ma'am."

An extremely pregnant Ruth Stanley was sitting on a sofa talking to her father and mother in-law, David and Edith Stanley. Judge Stanley rose easily, while Ruth braced herself against the arm of the sofa and rose with difficulty.

"Marshal Clay Best, what a surprise!" she said, offering her hand to Clay.

"No, the pleasure is all ours," Clay said, bowing slightly.

"Now, what's this about Mr. and Mrs. Clay best?" Ruth said with a grin.

"It is true, *señora*. *Señor* Clay and I were married after we saw your grandfather," Teresa said. "Now, we are going to have a little *nene* like you."

Ruth leaned to kiss Teresa's cheek. "My father-in-law insists that our baby is going to be a girl. What does Clay have his heart set on? A boy or a girl?"

"My husband says he doesn't care, but I think a boy will make him happy. And I shall name him Clay, after his father."

"Actually, I really don't care either way, just as long as it has all its parts and is healthy. What do you think, Judge?" Clay said.

"Amen to that." David Stanley poured three glasses of brandy, handing one to Clay and a second to Edith. He then poured two cups of tea, handing them to the pregnant women. "Here's to the prettiest and smartest children in the great state of Texas." He held his glass of brandy high in a toast.

"Amen," Clay said.

Clay sipped his brandy, then set the glass on the coffee table and cleared his throat.

"Ma'am, what we actually came here for isn't exactly pleasant."

"Oh?" Ruth sat her cup on the table. "I suppose it concerns my grandfather Lester?"

"Yes ma'am, it does."

"Is he dead?"

"Yes ma'am, I'm afraid so."

"I see." She sat on the sofa and looked up at Clay with moist eyes. "How did it happen?"

"An Apache war party raided Cool Water. It seems your grandfather was there by himself. They killed him. Teresa and me came along later and found him. We buried him in the cemetery, and Teresa said some prayers over him."

"Oh, God," Ruth said with a sob and covered her mouth with a handkerchief. "What happened? I mean, why was he there alone?"

"Well, ma'am, the town died, plain and simple. With the drought and rustlers taking all he had, everyone just packed up and left. There wasn't nothing to hold them. And you know how stubborn your grandpa was. Cool Water was his town, and he wasn't gonna leave it, no matter what."

"Now, I guess he will never leave it. Will he?" She sniffled and shook her head.

"No ma'am, In a way, he got his dream. Cool Water will always be his."

The front door opened and closed as Ruth's husband, Buford, entered. He paused at the parlor and smiled.

"Well, well, well. If it isn't Marshall Clay Best. It is good to see you again." He gave Clay's hand a vigorous shake. "What brings you to San Antonio?"

"Marshall Best was just giving Ruth some sad news," David said. "Ruth's grandfather was murdered by an Apache raiding party."

"Ahh no," Buford sat beside Ruth and put an arm around her shoulders. "I am so sorry, honey."

"They also burnt the town to the ground," Clay said. "All except the saloon and my old house. They tried to burn my place, but I reckon there might've been too much Texas dust, and it just wouldn't burn."

"Did they burn grandpa's house also?"

"Yes ma'am, I'm afraid so."

"Oh, God," she said, shaking her head. "He's really gone, and I wasn't there to tell him I loved him, even as mean and nasty as he was."

"I figure he knew that, ma'am. 'Cause you always seemed to love everyone, even the ornery ones."

Yolanda entered and gave a slight curtsy. "I took the liberty to set two extra places for your guests.

"Oh, no need of that, ma'am," Clay said quickly. "We didn't mean to come barging in on you at dinner time."

"Nonsense," Buford said. "We would be insulted if you didn't dine with us. I don't have to be back in court until two o'clock. We'll have plenty of time to visit.

******

"Marshall Clay married Teresa after their last visit," Ruth said.

"Really?" Buford laid his fork in his plate and staring at Teresa. "What in the world made you marry him?"

"My husband is only teasing you," Ruth said at the confused expression on Teresa's face.

"Oh," Teresa nodded. "I don't know. Sometimes I wonder."

"Now, they are going to have a baby also," Edith Stanley said softly. It seems as if it is contagious."

"Just don't you get any ideas," David said.

"Don't worry, I believe we are well past that point." Edith laughed. "Now, I plan to spoil the dickens out of our grandchildren."

"How's the trial coming," David asked, changing the subject.

"It could be a short one," Buford said. "The defense hasn't presented much of a case, and the prosecution has covered every aspect possible. The only thing they don't have is a photograph of him killing his wife."

"My son is presiding over a murder trial," David said, leaning to look at Clay. "It seems the manager of a large department store was having an affair with a younger woman. His wife refused to give him a divorce, so he bludgeoned her to death with a fireplace poker and ransacked the house to make it look like a burglary gone bad."

"Well, if he did it, he deserves to get hung," Clay said.

"Why don't we talk about something more pleasant," Ruth said.

"Yes, please," Edith said.

"Well, I reckon now's about as good a time as any to tell Ruth a bit of news you all might be interested in," Clay said. "It seems your grandpa Les had a will, leaving everything to you."

"I beg your pardon?" Ruth said.

"I asked Henry Jenkins at the bank in Carrizo Springs to do some checking, and he discovered that Les had filed a legal will, leaving the Cool Water ranch and all it's holdings to you, his granddaughter."

"But didn't you say that the Indians had burnt Cool Water to the ground?" Ruth said.

"Yes ma'am, but he had a copy of the will stored in a safety deposit box in Henry's bank. He must've had a premonition of something going wrong. The fact is, the Indians burnt the buildings, but not the land. You own one thousand acres of Texas ranch land. He did owe some folks some money for other things, but the land was paid for."

"How much did he owe?" Buford asked.

"Oh, I don't rightly know, but I can find out. It doesn't amount to a whole lot, mostly just back wages to folks that worked for him. He owed me a thousand dollars, but I've already given up on that months ago."

"Well, what do you think of that news, honey?" Buford said with a chuckle. You are the proud owner of a ranch. What are you going to do with it?"

"You could rebuild the house and move back there," Clay said. "You could run the ranch, and your husband could practice law in Carrizo Springs."

"I don't want any part of that place," Ruth said, shaking her head. "It holds nothing but bad memories for me."

"Well, do you want to sell it?" David asked.

"I don't care. Sell it, or give it to Marshal Best. You said he owed you some money," she said to Clay. "Take the land as payment."

Clay laughed and took a sip of water. "That land is worth a site more than what your grandpa owed me, even with this drought. I asked Henry to check on the value, and he said that, even with the buildings being destroyed, and with the drought, the land is still worth about $15.00 an acre. That means your Cool Water ranch is worth $15,000.00. That's a whole lot more than what Les owed me."

Ruth stared at Clay opened-mouthed.

"So, what do you think?" Buford asked after a pregnant moment.

"I, I, I don't know."

"Let me make this easy," Clay said. "Teresa and me came into a bit of money, and I'd like to buy the place, if you're willing to sell. And you folks would be welcome to come visit anytime you want."

"$15,000.00 is a lot of money, Mr. Best. What terms are you wishing to make? A down payment with interest?" David asked.

"No, I've got me a bank draft for $15,000.00 right here in my pocket, with the deed. I mean to pay for what I buy."

"Do you mind my asking where a man like you would have access to that amount of money," Buford said.

"Like I said, me and Teresa came into some money. We also have two men who are going to be partners in this ranching venture. We hope to buy some more land. That is, if Mrs. Stanley is willing to sell."

"Marshall Best, you and June were the only real friends I had when I lived in Cool Water. I don't know how many times I cried on your shoulder, and ate at your table. I am willing to give you the land, free and clear. You and June are the only pleasant memories I have of the place. Please, take it."

Clay pulled a pack of folded papers from his inside coat pocket and slid them across the table.

"Just sign the deed, Mrs. Stanley, and I'll do just that."

Buford Stanley opened the packet and quickly thumbed through the papers. "You thought of everything, didn't you?"

"Yes sir, and I aim to treat Mrs. Stanley right. The check is made out to her."

"Yes, it is. Please excuse me for a moment."

He rose from the table and returned a minute later with an ink well and pen.

"Sign here...and here..."

Clay squeezed Teresa's hand under the table as she smiled.

******

"Well, how do you feel, being the owner of a large cattle ranch?" Clay removed his tie as Teresa pulled her dress over her head. She shook her head and combed her long hair back with her fingers before answering.

"*We* are owners. You and I own part, Leo and his wife own 20%, and Julio and Estrella also own 20%." She pulled the tie on her petticoats and let them fall to the floor.

"Yeah, but we own 60%. I ain't going to go through this much trouble and let them tell me what to do."

He watched silently as she removed the rest of her garments and grabbed her thin nightgown. She studied it for a few seconds before casting it aside. She lay on the bed with both hands tucked behind her head and smiled.

"Come here, and I'll show you how I feel."

"Are you up for it?" Clay felt his knees go weak.

"*Carumba, marido muy fuerte.* I am going to have a baby. I am not an invalid. Come here."

"Oh, yeah," he said and slid into her open arms.

Chapter 52

Manuel tied Miguel's horse in the brush and climbed slowly onto a ledge of rock, overlooking the road to Carrizo Springs. He was not fully healed, but the pain in his left shoulder and foot were nothing compared to the festering inside his stomach. The only way he could heal that festering was to see the dead bodies of Clay Best and Teresa.

He blew the dust off the trigger of the Henry repeating rifle and injected a round into the chamber.

It had been easy to learn where the gringo lived. Taking a lesson from Leo Santiago on how to find information without attracting attention, he had ridden into Carrizo Springs quietly three days earlier. He casually mentioned to the man running the stables that he was a friend of Marshal Clay Best, and heard that he lived in Carrizo Springs. He quickly discovered that Clay and Teresa did live there. They had somehow come into a great amount of money, and had gone to San Antonio to see the woman who owned the Cool Water Ranch south of Carrizo Springs. They were hoping to buy it. They were expected to arrive any day now.

Hoping to get a more accurate time of their return, Manuel spent the next two days lounging in the cantina and drinking *cerveza*. It was late in the afternoon of the second day that a big man with a star pinned on his vest came in and ordered a mug of *cerveza*. The bartender asked about Clay and Teresa Best, and Manuel held his mug to his lips and listened without swallowing. The sheriff said he had received a telegram that they should arrive the next day by buggy. Manuel smiled as he finished his beer.

Manuel spent the night in a stall inside the stable. He paid his bill early in the morning and rode quietly out of town. He spied the pile of boulders about eight miles north of town and rode off into the brush and cactus.

Manuel eased the hammer down on the loaded chamber and made himself comfortable. He had a clear vision of the road. Clay and Teresa Best were his. He would end the festering that afternoon. He toasted the empty road with a bottle of whiskey before pulling the cork.

Chapter 53

Teresa grabbed the edge of the seat and frowned as the buggy jolted over a rut in the road.

"Tell me one more time. Why are we riding in this thing, when I could be riding Diablo?"

"Because you're going to have our baby, and I don't want anything to happen to it," Clay said, giving the reins a shake. The team of dappled greys were a fine-looking pair, but they needed constant reminding that they were supposed to be moving forward, and not standing still.

"I'll tell you what's going to happen. I am going to shoot you, if you tell me I'm going to have a baby one more time. That is what's going to happen."

She folded her arms and glared at the road ahead. They were approximately eight miles from Carrizo Springs, and the thought of a cool bath and change of clothing were ranking pretty high at the moment. Worst of all, their horses, Diablo and Loco, were tied to the back of the uncomfortable contraption she was being forced to ride in.

"We should be there by mid-afternoon," Clay said.

"We could already be there, if we were riding the horses."

"Yeah, but..." He stopped as she jerked around to glare. "Point well taken."

He gave the reins another shake.

They were nearing a pile of boulders when one of the horses dropped to the ground simultaneously with the report of a rifle.

"Out!" Clay yelled. He grabbed for Teresa's arm, but she was already bailing from the buggy on the opposite side. A second shot dropped the other horse. Clay dove from the buggy and quickly untied Loco and Diablo. Jerking his Winchester from the scabbard, he swatted both animals on the rump. "Ya!" They bolted off the road and into the brush. Another shot kicked up dust near his feet as he ducked behind the buggy.

"Are you okay?" he yelled as another shot kicked dust near the rear wheel.

"*Sí*, I am fine," she said from beneath the buggy. "Who is shooting at us?"

"I don't know. Must be someone I offended at one time or other." He levered a round into the chamber and slid another into the magazine.

"Hey, gringo. How do you like hiding behind your woman? Huh, gringo?"

"Manuel Rosales," Clay said quietly to Teresa. "Dammit! I should've made sure he was dead."

"Hey, gringo. I'm going to kill you and your woman."

"I thought I'd killed you awhile back, Manuel," Clay yelled. "You were bleeding like a stuck hog. How'd you get away?"

"Ah...you should know, gringo, that Manuel Rosales does not die so easily. I always come back and make people pay for what they've done."

Clay could feel the heat from the sunbaked road burning through the knees of his pants as sweat trickled from beneath his hat and down his cheeks. He looked at Teresa as she rubbed her palms against her dress.

"You've caught us at a disadvantage, Manuel. What do you want?" Clay yelled.

"What do I want?" Manuel laughed loudly. "You shot me, so now I will shoot you. But not before I make you suffer. I will shoot Teresa first. How do you like that, gringo? Huh?"

"I don't care for it at all," Clay yelled. "Teresa's going to have a baby, so I'm asking you to let her go. Then, after she's gone, you and me can finish this deal like a couple of men."

Manuel laughed again. "You must think Manuel Rosales is *estúpido*. No, Teresa will die first. Then, after you've seen her dead, then I will kill you, gringo, real slow."

Clay lay flat next to Teresa as several more shots from Manuel's rifle ripped through the buggy, kicking up dust inches from his boots.

"He's playing a game," Clay said. "He could kill us anytime he wants, but he's got us cooking the life out of ourselves in this heat, with our canteen still inside the buggy." He looked at Teresa as she mopped her face with her handkerchief.

"You've really got to be miserable with all them petticoats on."

"*Sí*, but there is no room to take them off," she said with a grin.

Clay studied the boulders as Manuel fired several more shots. A haze of blue smoke hung over one particular boulder in the middle of the pile. Another puff of smoke appeared as a brass cartridge bounced down the face of the rock with a tinkle.

"He ain't particularly smart, is he?"

"Manuel Rosales? No," Teresa said, shaking her head. "No one has ever accused him of being smart. Why?"

"He just gave away his position. Well, I for one, ain't standing for much more of this. Here," Clay said, passing the Winchester to Teresa. He scooted close to her and pointed toward the boulders.

"See that small indentation toward the middle?"

"Where?" She placed her head against his arm.

"There, on the top, near the middle of the pile."

He had no more gotten the words out when another puff of smoke appeared and a bullet ripped through the buggy.

"*Sí*, I do now."

"Good. When I give the word, I want you to aim for that spot and empty the gun. Fire each round about two seconds apart, and aim about a foot high. Got that?"

"*Sí*."

"With any luck, we'll put an end to Manuel Rosales once and for all." He reached into his jacket pocket and handed her more bullets. "Take these in case you need them."

Clay slid backwards from beneath the buggy and removed his black jacket, casting it aside. It was covered with dirt. He pulled the .45 from the holster and checked the rounds, then repeated the process with the .38 Colt he kept tucked in his belt.

"Now!" he yelled as another bullet ripped through the buggy. He darted off the road and into the brush as Teresa began firing. He glanced at the boulders in time to see one of her bullets kick up a small cloud of dust as it ricocheted off the rock Manuel had been firing from. Clay jumped into a wash approximately twenty-five yards from the boulders as Teresa emptied the rifle. There was a lull in the noise as she reloaded.

"That was clever, gringo!" Manuel yelled. "But I am still alive." He fired several shots at the buggy.

Damn fool doesn't know I'm here. Clay slipped quietly forward, inching through the brush until he reached the first boulder. He heaved a sigh of relief as Teresa fired several more shots that whined off the boulders above his head.

Okay, let's put an end to this fiasco.

Cocking his .45, Clay worked his way around the boulder. On a ledge of granite, approximately ten foot off the sand, Manuel Rosales stood with his back toward Clay, feeding bullets into his rifle.

"Hey, gringo. It does no good to waste good ammunition. You can't kill me, gringo. But I shall kill you."

Clay aimed and pulled the trigger. The slug slammed into Manuel's right leg, spinning him off the ledge and sending the rifle into a clump of greasewood.

"I don't think I'm gonna let you kill me today," Clay said calmly as he approached. "You should've known I wouldn't die so easily either."

Manuel blinked the dust from his eyes and scooted backward.

"How did...? I..." he said, glancing toward the boulders.

"Teresa doesn't quit either." Clay said. He turned as the sound of boots against gravel rounded the base of the boulders. Teresa appeared, gripping the rifle in her hands.

Manuel cursed loudly as he drew his pistol and fired. Clay drug Teresa to the ground as Manuel's bullet bounced off the boulders with a whine. Rolling to one knee, Clay fired twice. Both bullets hit Manuel in the chest, knocking him flat.

Teresa scooted against his legs as Clay stood. He waited a few seconds, then circled through the brush and approached Manuel's head.

"Is he dead this time?" she asked.

"If he ain't, he's gonna be," Clay said, cocking his pistol.

He kicked Manuel's gun aside and fired the last three bullets into his body. Teresa cocked the Winchester and fired her last round into his head.

"I think that should do. He's dead," she said with a nod.

"I'll say." Clay glanced at her as he reloaded the Colt. "The odd part was that he was by his lonesome. I figure no one else was stupid enough to come with him."

"Lucky for them," Teresa said.

Chapter 54

It had been five months since the demise of Manuel Rosales and Clay was enjoying the quiet pace Carrizo Springs had to offer. He had gotten back into the habit of rising at dawn, making coffee and feeding Antonio his breakfast. He would then pour two mugs of coffee and rejoin Teresa in bed. According to Doc Phillips, she was only weeks away from giving birth. The thought both excited and frightened Clay. He had no idea how to be a proper father. His own father had not been any great shakes of a dad, and Clay figured he ought to work at being a better father. He had asked advice from every dad in Carrizo Springs, and tried his best to cypher what he'd learned.

"You just do the best you can," Ray King said with a chuckle. "There's no handbook on the subject."

"Yeah, but it looks like you're doing pretty damned good, Ray. How'd you learn to do it?"

"How'd I learn? I don't figure I've *learned* much of anything. I listen to Maria a lot. But mostly, I love the boys and spend time with them. That's about all a man can do."

He was still anxious at the thought, and came to the conclusion that every man he'd talked to had felt the same way. Many of them still felt that way, even when their children were grown. One particular friend, who had a thirteen-year-old daughter, said he was more nervous now than when she was a baby. That thought didn't make Clay feel any better, and he didn't know what he'd do if Teresa had a girl. He figured that what he was facing was just plain hell either way.

He held Teresa's arm as she waddled down the wooden walkway and entered the general store.

"Oh, Clay, I'm glad you and Mrs. Best came in," James Rolling said from behind the counter. "I have a couple of letters for you."

"Letters? Who'd be writing us?" Clay said.

"I don't know, but..." he pulled two envelopes from a cubby on the wall behind the counter, "here they are. One addressed to Miss Teresa Romero of Carrizo Springs, and another with the same handwriting, addressed to Marshal Clay Best, of Cool Water, Texas."

"How'd you wind up with mail for Cool Water," Clay said, taking the envelopes.

"All the mail for Cool Water comes here. Not so much since it burnt to the ground, but they never had a post office, so Les used to pop in once a week to collect his mail. Now, if anything arrives, I just send it back on the next stage. All except those two. I thought you ought to get them."

"Much obliged," Clay mumbled, studying the envelopes. He passed the one addressed to Teresa and she promptly gave it back.

"Read it."

"Well, it's yours. You ought to read it."

"Read it," she repeated.

Clay stared at her for a few seconds before realizing the woman he had married could not read.

"Oh, yeah," he said, tearing open the envelope. He glanced over the neat handwriting and cleared his throat.

"It's from your friend Rob Mayfield."

"Rob?" she asked excitedly. "What does he say?"

Dear Miss Romero,

I hope this letter finds you well and in good health. I have fond memories of Carrizo Springs, and will always cherish my time there, especially meeting and knowing you.

I am sure by now you have heard that my brother, Billy, got killed while robbing the bank at Cool Water.

Thankfully, I was not with him, and would not have participated in such a deed. I left shortly after seeing him buried, and returned to Pittsburg, Texas, and to Clara Jean Russell. You will remember my telling you about her, and how I loved her. Clara Jean and I were married, and now have a three-month-old son named Joshua.

The reason I am writing this letter is to inform you that the drought has finally taken a firm hold on the Russell farm, and the last cotton crop was not enough to pay for itself. This left Clara's parents deep in debt, and the bank is seeking to repossess the entire farm. It also seems that the men who killed Billy have relatives here in Pittsburg who are carrying a grudge. Several attempts have been made on our lives. Clara's family and I are pulling up stakes like many families, and leaving Texas. Mr. Russell is looking to move his family to California, in the hope of starting over. I have begged and pleaded that we visit my brother's grave in Cool Water, and they have kindly agreed, although it will add several days to our journey.

We are now packed, and will be leaving tomorrow at daybreak. I will mail this letter in the first town we pass through, knowing it will arrive much quicker than we will. I hope to see you at that time and introduce you to my wife and son.
Sincerely yours,
Rob Mayfield

Clay studied his wife for a few seconds while she stared at the letter in his hands.

"They are coming here?"

"That's what he says."

"Where will they stay?"

"Well, I reckon that's up to them," Clay said with a chuckle. "They'll likely only be here a few days, then move on."

"Why?"

"Why what?"

"Why will they only be here a few days?" Teresa snapped.

"Because he says so right here." He waved the letter in the air. "They're moving to California."

"Why? Why do they have to go to California, when there is so much land right here?"

"My hell, Teresa, how am I supposed to know? You can ask them that when they get here."

"What does your letter say?"

"Give me a chance to read it, and I'll let you know."

Clay tore the envelope open and quickly read it to himself. "It says they are coming, and he wants to visit Billy's grave. Plain and simple." He stuffed both letters back in their envelopes.

"Now, can we get what we came for and head back home, before you have that baby in Jim's store?"

Teresa followed Clay as he walked the isles, placing items in a basket.

"Rob is a nice boy and works hard. We have plenty of land. We'll need more vaqueros who will want to eat. Rob could grow chilies, and cilantro, and..."

"Because they want their own farm. Besides, the drought is here also, and it's hard to grow anything without water."

"But it will rain soon. They should stay here."

"Teresa," Clay said, laying the basket on the floor. He took her cheeks in his palms and kissed her nose. "You can tell Rob and his wife exactly that, when they get here. Okay?"

"*Bien.*" She grinned and kissed him back.

End

About The Authors

MAJOR MITCHELL (pictured on the left), is the author of ten novels and two children's books. He lives with his wife, Judy, in Northern California. A member of The Western Writers of America and a frequent guest speaker at historical meetings and schools on the west coast, he has also written several songs, and takes the stage on rare occasions as a singer.

JERRY MITCHELL (pictured on the right), is the author of several short stories, a book of poetry and has co-written three novels with his brother. He lives with this wife, Juana, in Northern California, approximately 45 minutes from his brother Major. His ideas have been the inspiration for four of Major's novels. More about the authors, their books and photo gallery may be found at www.majormitchell.net.
Correspondence for both authors should be addressed to:
Shalako Press
P.O. Box 371
Oakdale, CA 95361-0371
http://www.shalakopress.com

Other Books By Major Mitchell

The Doña

Mokelumne Gold

Poverty Flat

Dusty Boots (with Jerry Mitchell)

Joker's Play (with Jerry Mitchell)

A Reason To Believe

Canyon Wind

Manhunter

Where The Green Grass Grows

Please visit our online bookstore at:
www.shalakopress.com